THE GROWN-UP

THE GROWN-UP

A THRILLER

TRANSLATED BY JAI VAN ESSEN

SASKIA NOORT

This is a work of fiction. Names, characters, organizations, places, events, and incidents are either products of the author's imagination or are used fictitiously. Any resemblance to actual persons, living or dead, or actual events is purely coincidental.

Text copyright © 2021, 2025 by Saskia Noort
Translation copyright © 2025 by Jai van Essen
All rights reserved.

No part of this book may be reproduced, or stored in a retrieval system, or transmitted in any form or by any means, electronic, mechanical, photocopying, recording, or otherwise, without express written permission of the publisher.

Previously published as *Bonuskind* by The House of Books in The Netherlands in 2021. Translated from Dutch by Jai van Essen. First published in English by Amazon Crossing in 2025.

Published by Amazon Crossing, Seattle

www.apub.com

Amazon, the Amazon logo, and Amazon Crossing are trademarks of Amazon.com, Inc., or its affiliates.

EU product safety contact:
Amazon Media EU S. à r.l.
38, avenue John F. Kennedy, L-1855 Luxembourg
amazonpublishing-gpsr@amazon.com

ISBN-13: 9781662525339 (paperback)
ISBN-13: 9781662525346 (digital)

Cover design by Brian Lemus
Cover image: © Alena Veasey, © Vladimir Gjorgiev / Shutterstock

Printed in the United States of America

THE GROWN-UP

1.

Mom's dead. It's my first thought when I open my eyes. What did I dream that made me think this? I only remember snippets. A door slammed shut somewhere in our old home, Dad still there. Hissing whispers, the way they acted those last months together. A car, screeching tires. Was all this a dream or something else?

I switch on the lamp beside my bed, reach for the glass of water that's always there, and finish it. I feel hot and cold at the same time. Maybe I'm sick. I'd like to go to Mom's room, but I'm afraid to. I reach for my cell phone and check my messages on WhatsApp. Nothing.

I feel scared. Of so many things. That Mom really is dead. That I might have a bladder infection again. That Mees will ignore me at school. That my little brother, Luuk, and I will have to go live with Dad, that Mom is out of money, and we'll have to live on the streets. I have no idea what brought these fears on. I feel like I can't breathe, like there's something wrong with the air in this house. Carbon monoxide. I imagine that Mom and Luuk and our Labradoodle mix, Chonk, are dead already, and that if I don't get out of bed to open my window I'll die too. I'm dizzy as I think about all those news stories about family murders, think for a second that maybe Mom drugged me and Luuk, but I also remember what my Dutch teacher said: that I have an overly wild imagination, and sometimes he's concerned about me. "Your parents need to realize they're damaging their children with their arguing."

I tiptoe out of bed and open the window. The cold night air calms me. Everything's alright, of course. The streets are dark and quiet. Mom's car is parked outside the door, and Luuk's bicycle is in the yard. I'm just afraid of our new life here in this windy neighborhood without grass or trees, right by the motorway. I can think things at night that I wouldn't say during the day. For example, I'd like to tell my Dutch teacher that his opinion isn't helping either. I'm well aware my parents are damaging us, just like I also know they're not doing it on purpose. But what can Luuk and I do? We're caught in the middle. We listen, we keep silent, we wait. We pack our bags each week and make sure we have everything we need with us, otherwise all hell breaks loose. We've become our parents' parents. We manage their emotions, soothe their anger, maneuver past their hatred. Best not to bother them with our needs, since the slightest ripple leads to yet another battle in the war.

I crawl back into bed and curl up, my hands between my knees.

I tell myself that everything's alright.

2.

I get in the car, and when he leans in to kiss me, I cringe. He pretends not to notice I'm being standoffish, but I can tell he's annoyed by the way he works the gas pedal.

"So tell me," he says, speeding through the traffic-calmed streets of our neighborhood, which is still under construction. "Why the big rush to meet?"

"Could you please drive slower? We don't need to go anywhere. Let's park and talk in the car."

"It's a bit cold, isn't it? I'm nearly freezing."

I want this over with. I don't want him anywhere near my children. I don't want to be alone with him in my house either.

He makes a left onto the main road and starts driving even faster. I start to reach for my phone but realize I've left it at home.

"Please, could you slow down?"

I know better than to ask that. The dumbest thing I can do with him is show any sign of fear.

He laughs and pushes the car to seventy miles per hour.

"There could be children riding without lights on their bikes. Or people out walking their dogs."

"Well, that would be very stupid of them, in the dead of night on an unlit road." He puts his hand on my knee. "Are you scared?"

"Yes," I say.

"Oh, sweet Twigs, you don't need to be afraid of anything."

He abruptly slams the brakes and stops the car by the side of the road. "Alright, then. What is it you want to tell me?"

I put my cold hand on my feverish forehead. I've hardly slept for days, weeks. I'm so tired I can't think straight anymore.

"I'm confused," I say. It's not true. I was confused for a long time, but now I'm quite certain.

"Confused about what? Me? About us? That's to be expected, isn't it? This thing between us is huge. The Champions League pales in comparison."

"I'm neglecting my children; my work and health are suffering. The games you play . . . I'm just not cut out for this."

Only now does he really look at me. His eyes are like glowing coals in the dark. He puts his face in his hands and takes a deep breath.

"Games I play . . . Don't underestimate yourself, Twigs. But what exactly are you trying to say?"

It's like my brain is shrinking to the size of a raisin. This happens every time I'm with him. My mouth is dry, my hands clammy. I'd like nothing more than to jump in his lap and ask him to forgive me. But forgive me for what? I have no idea. I only know that he makes me feel like I'm stupid and like I'm doing everything wrong all the time.

"This relationship isn't good for me," I manage to squeeze out.

"'Relationship'?"

"Well, this. Whatever it is we have."

"This is a relationship to you?"

That's the moment he takes charge of the conversation. He's found my weakness and is using it against me.

"Whatever you want to call it, I'm ending it."

Well done, I tell myself. It doesn't matter how the rest of the conversation goes, so long as the result is this is over.

He starts to laugh. "Oh, dear Twigs."

What kind of person refers to his lover as a twig?

He tries to put his arm around me. I flinch at his touch, like I've gotten an electric shock.

The Grown-Up

"My God. You're not really afraid of me, are you?"

My fear borders on panic now. And yet I still let him take the lead. I've completely lost control of the situation.

"Listen," I say, starting the sermon I've been rehearsing for weeks. "I'm breaking up with you. I mean it this time. It's over. And if you have any feelings for me at all, you'll respect that. So no more calling or messaging or just showing up at my door. I need peace. I need to be there for my children. I'm sorry, this is all just too much for me."

He rests his head on the steering wheel. My hand moves toward the car door. I try to open it, but he's locked it.

"What are you trying to do, Sticks? Did you think you could just dump me by the side of the road? My God!"

He starts the car again and hits the gas, making the engine roar. I tell myself I'm to blame for whatever happens now. I can see my children's faces before me as babies, toddlers, and as they are now: adolescent and prepubescent. I see their gangly awkwardness and almost smell them, their sweat mixed with deodorant.

"Please, take me home. The kids are all alone. I need to go home."

"You and your goddamn kids all the time. Why do you use them as an excuse? If you don't want to see me anymore, just say so."

"We've discussed this a thousand times. I don't want to introduce them to a new man until I'm sure they're up for it. They have enough to deal with already. And what you and I have . . . You've said it yourself: this isn't a relationship. It's something intensely sick, toxic . . . a kind of virus. Or a psychosis. Sometimes that's what I think: that you don't even really exist."

I'm talking fast, as if by doing so I can get him to drive more calmly. As if anything I say could possibly get through to him. We exit the main road onto a narrower one and bounce over its bumps and potholes. There's no way he'll hurt me, I tell myself. This is God. I know him. He's an odd person, and I need to get rid of him, but this isn't some Netflix show. He'll stop sooner or later, and then we'll argue. After that we'll have sex, and then I'll get him to bring me home. He's a good person in the end.

3.

Every morning, I wake to the sound of my mother turning on the radio. She can't stand the quiet. But I don't hear anything today, which is odd. I check my phone. Twenty-one WhatsApp messages, not one of them from her. There's one from Dad, though, sent at one o'clock last night.

Sleep tight, dear Lies. I miss you guys.

It's nine o'clock. My stomach is growling. Mom's out walking Chonk, no doubt.

I get up, slip my feet into my tiger slippers, and put on my robe: tiger print too. It crackles as I put it on. The fabric is synthetic as hell.

My brother's room is empty. I go downstairs. Luuk is still in his pajamas, sitting on the couch with headphones on, a game controller in hand. He smells sweet, like cookies.

I pull his headphones right off his head.

"Lies, you jerk!" He draws my name out to annoy me: *Leeez.*

"You're pathetic. Did Mom go out to walk Chonk?"

"I have no idea. *You're* pathetic."

The curtains are still drawn. There's a half-full glass of red wine on the table next to her laptop and an ashtray with a cigarette butt. Mom hasn't smoked in years. At least, that's what she claims. Maybe she had someone over for a visit. But if she did, then there would be two glasses.

I hear Chonk jumping up against the door to the pantry off the kitchen. I go free him, and he thanks me by barking and jumping all over me.

The Grown-Up

"There you are," I say. "So where's Mom, then?"

Chonk and I walk across the field. I'm wearing my mom's jogging suit, which I found lying at the foot end of her bed. I'd smelled her pillows and sheets to see if she'd spent the night there. The scent of her was strong, but it was hard to tell if that meant anything. *Don't get so carried away!* she often says to me. She says I have an overly wild imagination. I tell myself I'll come home in a little while, the table will be set, and she'll have picked up croissants. Or maybe she told me she had to go to work early, and I just forgot. Except her car is parked out front, and her bike is up against the fence. She can't have gone very far. I call her on my phone, but she doesn't answer.

It's cold out, and there's not a cloud in the sky. Chonk is jumping and running and rolling across the grass. He stops and relieves himself, behind the bushes, fortunately. I keep walking, thinking how strange all this is. I have my hand in one pocket and my phone in the other. Should I call Dad?

"That's a terrible idea." I can hear Mom say it. She and Dad hate each other. They don't say this. They say they wish each other all the best, but they disagree a lot, and it's clear they don't understand each other. Dad once said marrying Mom was the biggest mistake of his life.

"Are Luuk and I mistakes too, then?" I asked.

"No, of course not. You're the greatest thing that's ever happened to me."

That seemed odd. To be a mistake and the greatest thing ever at the same time. But I didn't say so, because these kinds of conversations always make me feel uncomfortable. That's why I don't call him. I don't want to give him an opportunity to talk bad about Mom.

I call her again. She's probably at work. Maybe one of her therapy patients, whom she calls clients, called her. Some emergency. Only if that were the case, she would have left a note or sent a text, saying so. Unless it was such a big emergency that she didn't have time? Suicide, psychosis . . . Mom's patients are crazy. *She's crazy too,* Dad says in my mind. I wish it would stop. Their voices in my head, fighting all the time.

She isn't home. No croissants, no note. I feed Chonk, make tea, and ask Luuk if he wants a grilled cheese sandwich. I butter the old bread and put cheese on it. Did I hear anything last night? The television, I remember that. You can hear everything in this house. Chonk was barking for a little while. Mom yelled at him to shut up. She came to kiss me good night, which I felt a bit awkward about. I'm not a child anymore. I'm seventeen. Mom said never mind that. She said I wouldn't find it silly someday. Said I'd be happy later to have these memories.

Luuk doesn't seem worried about anything. I want to keep it that way. I hand him his grilled cheese sandwich and tea with sliced banana on the side.

"I don't like banana," he says. "Don't you know that?"

"No," I say. "I don't." Is it strange not to know something like that? Luuk's a bit of shadow in our house. Mom had him tested, but it seems there's nothing wrong with him. He's just "different," she says. Dad thinks that's nonsense. He says it's Mom who made him different with all her psychologizing. Dad had him join a soccer club. Mom says Luuk might be gay. It's annoying how people always get labeled as one thing or another. If you ask me, Luuk's just Luuk.

I make myself some coffee and turn on the radio so it'll feel a bit like she's home. It's ten o'clock. I huddle up in her armchair and scroll through my phone. I barely glance at my friends' messages. Dad's shared a photo of me, Luuk, Laura—his girlfriend—and himself in the WhatsApp group he made for us four. I delete it. On Facebook Messenger, I see Mom was last online at half past ten. Laura's posted the same photo of us on Instagram. She added the caption "Happy Modern Family." Dad replied with a heart, and the other comments are from her family. *You deserve this, girl.* Did Mom see this? I feel an ache somewhere below my heart.

I call again and hear a phone ring in the hallway. For a moment, I think she's home. That she's just walked in, is taking off her coat, quickly fixing her messy blond curls in front of the mirror, fumbling through her pockets. I go to the front door. Her purse is hanging from the banister. I take her phone out.

At what point does something that seems wrong actually become wrong? Maybe she's having coffee with someone down the street. That would be odd, though, since we've only just moved here.

"Luuk! Stop for a second."

I turn off the TV with the remote. A zombie stares back at me.

"Have you seen Mom?" I ask.

"No. Isn't she in bed?"

I shake my head.

"I'm sure she's somewhere."

"Right." I don't want to frighten him.

"I saw her last night," Luuk says. "She came into my room and kissed me."

"Me too. Did she say anything to you?"

"Just good night."

"Did she act different at all?"

"No. I don't know. She seemed the same as always."

I want to call someone, but if I do that then all this will be real. Or maybe they'll say I'm getting worked up over nothing. And who would I call anyway? My friend Evi with her perfect parents who worry about me and constantly say that the way my parents act isn't normal? What if they get Youth Care involved? Mom says that's the worst that could happen.

Last week while he was playing soccer, Luuk got hit in the head with a ball and had to go to the hospital. Dad couldn't reach Mom, so I found myself standing there in the hallway with Laura. She put her arm around me and kept talking to me like I was three years old. I felt sick from the smell of her perfume and cigarettes, from the way she talked to me in that baby voice of hers. I hated her for going to get soup and for stroking Dad's cheek while he talked on the phone. Then Mom arrived.

Laura started playing the diplomat when Mom and Dad went at each other over which of them was the most worthless parent.

Luuk turned out to be alright. He had a concussion and was allowed to go home. But the arguing continued: Who was taking Luuk home? Mom won. In the car, she said I'd reached the age where I could choose who I wanted to live with. "With both of you," I said, and she said: "Of course, sweetie. I understand."

Only she doesn't understand.

4.

Evi and I take Chonk for a walk. I don't know if I should tell her about my mother. If I do, she'll tell her own mom, and before you know it, things will be spinning out of control.
We'll come home in a little while, and she'll be there, I'm sure of it.
Evi pulls a small bottle out of her purse.
"What's that?"
"Cuarenta y Tres. It's so good."
We each take a sip of the Spanish liqueur. It's so sweet it makes my gums ache.
"Does your mother have a new boyfriend?"
"I don't think so. Why's that?"
"My father saw her, with a man."
"So? She's with men all the time for her work."
Maybe she's in the hospital. Suppose she was in a car crash, or fell? Or maybe she was bitten by a dog and someone took her to the hospital? I grab the bottle from Evi's hand and finish it. What if Mom's lying unconscious somewhere? My hands are turning clammy.
Evi's phone buzzes and she reads a text. "Is it alright if Malou joins us?"
I can't stand Malou. "No," I say, "I'd rather she didn't."
"Why are you acting so weird?"
"I'm not acting weird. What's weird about it? You know I don't like Malou. Why are you even asking? You're the one acting weird."

"Fine, I'm sorry. I only told you what my father said. No need to get mad at me. You're just upset because Mees is ignoring you."

Mees is the boy I kissed recently. I've been avoiding him ever since. But not because I don't like him. Quite the opposite.

"I'm the one ignoring him."

"Yeah, right."

Luuk's in tears when we come home.

"Where were you? I've been calling you this whole time."

"We just went out to walk Chonk. I'm home now."

I want Evi to leave.

"Dad called."

"What did you say?"

"That you were gone and so was Mom."

"And what did he say to that?"

"He's coming here."

"I'm leaving," Evi says, and she does.

I call Dad. It's not a good idea for him to come here. That'll only make things worse. Luuk and I can manage, and I'm sure Mom will be back shortly. I feel it. This happens to me all the time: I'll know in advance if something will be alright or if it won't, just like I also always know right away when someone's lying. Mom and Dad lie constantly.

"Lies, where are you?" he asks.

"At home. Luuk was just making a bit of a fuss."

"That was more than a bit. He's really upset."

"Not anymore."

"Whatever. I'm in the car and coming to get you."

"That isn't necessary."

"Where's your mother? Let me speak to her."

"She doesn't want to talk to you."

Lying. I'm better at it than grown-ups are.

"Why isn't she answering her phone?"

"Because she doesn't want to talk to you."

"I can't believe she left you two alone all night. Dammit! And she's always griping about what a bad father I am."

"Maybe you should calm down, Dad."

"Listen. Tell her I'm turning back for now, but my patience has run out. One more stunt like this and you're coming to live with me. Tell her it's time she got ahold of herself."

"Okay, Dad. We'll see you next week, okay?"

"You'll call, won't you? If anything's wrong, doesn't matter what time it is, call me and I'll come. Because I miss you two very much."

I hear him snuffle.

Oh, right, my mother's voice says. *That's what he does when he doesn't get what he wants. He gets all sentimental.*

I turn on Mom's laptop and enter the password. It's always the same: Chonk2017. I was right: the last thing she saw was Laura's post. I look at the photo once more. We're at the table at Dad's place. Laura's lifting Luuk onto her lap while I'm behind her next to Dad, who has his arm around me. Laura's used an extremely silly filter. She's one of those bunny- and bear-selfie people. I can hardly believe my father is dating someone like that.

I can guess what Mom's thinking: *My family. At my table. With my teapot. He's erased me.*

If she were here now, I'd comfort her and ask if she'd rather be sitting there instead.

No, she'd say. *Not for a single second.*

But she did see the photo. That's why she smoked a cigarette and disappeared. Even though we really weren't at all happy when the photo was taken, or certainly not as happy as we look, I knew it at the time: *Mom will see this, and she'll have a fit.* Why were we smiling so sweetly anyway? I don't know. It just happened. To make Dad happy, maybe? I have no idea.

My mother's a psychologist. Her bookcase is filled with books on problems. She has everything all figured out when it comes to other people. "Take a step back and observe yourself. Try to express your pain instead of losing yourself in it." She tells other people what to do, but she can't do it herself. She and Dad even argue over bathing suits. Luuk and I aren't to take ours to his house because Dad loses everything. "He'll just have to buy some swimsuits himself," she says. Luuk and I each have two bikes: one at Dad's place, one at Mom's. We celebrate two birthdays, two Saint Nicholases. Go on two vacations: to a camping site in Bakkum with her, to somewhere far away or an expensive ski resort with him. It's a competition for who's the best parent. They each tell their friends: *The kids do better with me.* Luuk and I don't say anything. It's best we don't. But more than anything, we wish we still had our old rooms, just one room each, in one neighborhood. Each of us with just one bicycle.

At home, Luuk and I eat fresh bread rolls with steak tartare and keep saying, "I'm sure she'll be back soon." We're probably overreacting. She'd never leave us behind like this. She can't live without us. It's a big misunderstanding. *Think about it for a second: Wasn't she taking a class today, spending a day at the spa, or meeting someone for a walk? Plus she has to go to Ikea to buy some final things for the house, and she said she'd be doing that this week.* But we always come back to the car, the purse, the phone.

I look for her passport in different drawers, bins, boxes, bags, under the mattress, and among her lingerie. When I lie down on her bed, her scent is so strong that for a moment I think she's back. I'm not going to cry. I need to keep a level head. I'm the mother for now. Not a mother like her, though. I won't let anger or self-pity drag me down. I'll think carefully and do what's best. No panic, no drama, no jumping to conclusions. She's out for a little while, but she'll be back.

After it's dark, I regret not going out to search while it was light out. I want to call the neighbors, but I don't have their number. Maybe Mom does. I grab her phone. The battery is almost dead. I plug in the charger and enter her PIN code: 1972, her birth year. She has a lot of messages on WhatsApp, including one in the Neighborhood Watch group, and early this morning she was called from an unidentified number.

The Grown-Up

Dear neighbors, last night around half past twelve, a black VW Golf was parked in front of number 74 with its engine running for quite some time. I didn't recognize the car as belonging to anyone on this street.

Below this an enlarged photo of the license plate, 44-XB-UW, followed by a message from somebody named Diets:

Ooh, scary! Better keep an eye out! Looks like some people have nothing better to do.

After that Diets left the group.

I don't know who Diets is, and there's only a phone number from whoever shared the photo.

My mother was last online at half past ten. The last time she messaged my father was four days ago. In her phone, he's called the Asshole.

How typical that all the underwear I bought for Lies recently didn't come back with her. Lies's teacher wants to talk to us at 3:40 this Thursday. Make sure you're there.

I often think back on the time when things were still good, or normal at least. The four of us at the table, or sleeping in on a Sunday. Watching TV in our pajamas. Driving in the car on vacation. Playing board games together, Dad's arm around Mom's shoulders. The two of them entertaining visitors, Mom cooking while Dad chatted and laughed. The one time I saw them dance at a wedding. Things weren't always bad between them, no matter what they say. Things were mostly good, or at least they were until Laura came along and ruined everything.

5.

I'm angry with Luuk for calling Dad. He has no idea how bad things are between those two. This call could cause Mom to lose custody. Dad's obsessively waiting for some mistake, some slipup, some moment of bad mothering he can jump at. And now he has one.

"What did he sound like?" I ask.

"I don't know."

"But what did he say?"

"'I'm coming right now.' That's all."

"You've ruined everything."

"Like what? Mom's gone—isn't that bad already?"

"Things will get even worse now."

I want to warn her, but I don't know how. I also want to say: *How could you do this? Are you happy now? Dad's coming to get us, and he'll never give us back.* He's going to play house with us and Laura, they'll have a baby together, and everyone will say: "Don't you think your father deserves this?" And I'll just nod and act fake. Or I'll be forced to choose and end up leaving Luuk with them. I'd rather live with Mom. She needs us the most. My room at Dad's place feels like someone else's room, some child Laura dreamed up, one who likes flowers and the color pink. I have no interest in big fluffy bears or Uggs with glitter on them. Laura always wants to take me shopping and get pedicures, but I'm not somebody's idea of a daughter who likes doing girly things.

The Grown-Up

I'm Lies. I like scary movies, hanging out with the boys, the color dark blue, sneakers, Billie Eilish, and hip-hop. And no, I'm not a lesbian, despite what some people at school say. That's why Mees kissed me. To test me, Evi said.

I'm so nervous I can't eat. Just like the night before Mom and Dad told us they were separating. I already knew. I'd sensed it coming for months, and that evening I heard them talking in the kitchen.

"We'll say we reached this decision together."

Mom was crying. "So you want me to lie?"

"Don't be dramatic."

"But this *is* dramatic."

"This isn't about what's good for us. It's about what's good for the children. We'll say we both decided it would be better if I go live somewhere else for a few months. That we still love each other very much but more as friends, not as husband and wife."

"What a load of crap."

"It's important we keep our emotions out of it."

"Fine. But one day they're going to see just what an ass you are."

"And what do you think they'll see when they look at you?"

There was a long silence, followed by sobbing.

"I rest my case."

One of them violently slammed the kitchen door.

That night, about two years ago now, was the night I got my first bladder infection. I didn't know what it was at the time. I kept having to pee, and it hurt, but I didn't want to make the situation with them even worse, so I didn't say anything. I googled the symptoms and read it helps to drink lots of water, so that's what I did, but it didn't work. The next day, while Dad was talking to us and Mom was crying, saying none of this was our fault, I got up and went to the bathroom and peed blood. At least the pain distracted me from what my parents were saying. Two days later, I woke up in a hospital bed with Mom and Dad by my side. That was my last happy moment.

Dad keeps his coat on and heads straight into the living room. I don't think he's ever been inside our house here. He looks around, breathing heavily.

"Come on, kids, get your things. I'm taking you home with me."

"We'll be fine right here," I say.

"Can't you stay here too?" Luuk asks him.

"I don't think your mother would approve."

"But shouldn't we go look for Mom?" Luuk says.

"We'll do that, sweetie. But I think Mom just needs a little space."

My parents say this a lot. At first Dad needed a little space, then Mom. Now there's tons of space between them, and it's still not enough.

"Dad," I say. "Shouldn't we call the police?"

"They won't do anything. Mom's a grown woman, and they only go looking for grown-ups after two weeks. There's no proof that anything's seriously wrong."

Dad's a lawyer, so he knows about things like this.

"She might have been in an accident," I say.

"Yeah, or been kidnapped," Luuk says.

"We'll call all the hospitals in the area, of course. Just leave that to us."

Us. Laura and him.

"Come on, guys, Laura's in the car."

"Why?"

"She's worried too."

Like I care. I don't say it, because it seems better not to argue right now. I wish so badly it was Laura who'd disappeared. Poof, gone. I wouldn't go looking for her, wouldn't call the police, wouldn't worry one second. All this started with her, and she can drop dead for all I care. The very thought of her makes me shiver. Even just her name. Laura. Did Luuk and I ask for her to come into our lives? Did we have a choice? And yet we're stuck with her every other week.

"Maybe you should ask Kim to help too," I say.

The Grown-Up

"And Grandma," Luuk adds.

"I think it's best if we don't worry Grandma just yet."

"Chonk needs to come with us," Luuk says.

Dad's face clouds over. He doesn't like pets. That's why Mom got us a puppy two years ago.

6.

Dad lives in a modern apartment building near his work. "This is what I always wanted," he said when he first showed it to us. Luuk and I each have a large bedroom with a double bed and our own television here. Laura decorated the place with some help from Pinterest. The whole apartment has gleaming white floors, and my bed stands on a kind of platform, where it's covered with big white and pink pillows. One has the word *HAPPY* embroidered onto it, the other says *GIRL*. Above the headboard, framed by Christmas lights, is a painting of two closed eyes with long eyelashes. All the rooms have tall glass doors, which looks nice but is rather inconvenient in terms of privacy. I covered mine with photos of my favorite musicians, and Luuk hung a flag of the Feyenoord soccer club in front of his. Dad's a rabid fan of Ajax, Feyenoord's biggest rival.

The kitchen is all black, with tall steel stools lining the kitchen island. An enormous gray lounge sofa sits in front of the gas heater, and when you press the remote the television rises from the floor.

Dad plops down beside us. "Put the phones away a minute, guys."

"I'm just checking if maybe Mom's online somewhere," Luuk says.

Her iPhone is in my purse, where I stashed it. As if I heard Mom tell me: *Don't let that jerk touch my phone.*

"How was Mom before she disappeared?" Dad asks.

My shoulders feel heavy. I always hate it when he asks these kinds of questions. Normally I'd say, "Ask her yourself." But I can't do that now.

The Grown-Up

"I don't know," Luuk says.

"Sad," I say. "She wasn't sleeping well, and she was tired a lot."

Dad nods and clenches his jaw. "Your mother gets a bit depressed sometimes. That's very unfortunate for her, but you two can't do anything about that. Nor can I. It's an illness. It's quite possible she went somewhere to clear her head. Laura and I are doing all we can to find her. We've also told Kim. Do you trust us? Don't worry, it's really going to be fine. When we find her, we'll make sure she gets the help she needs. Anyway, you're safe with us, and you can even decide where you'd like to eat tonight."

Eat. Like I'm in the mood.

"McDonald's," Luuk says. Laura hates McDonald's.

"Yeah," I say. "McDonald's!"

"Alright, McDonald's it is."

We drive through the quiet Buitenveldert neighborhood, and I see her in every woman we pass. I haven't told anyone about my dream yet. The feeling returns, here in this car smelling of Laura's strong perfume: Mom's dead. She's lying somewhere, cold and alone, and we're going to McDonald's.

I wish Luuk and I could talk to Dad about Mom, and vice versa. That we could say what we did and ate at the other parent's house, what Mom or Dad said, or what we laughed about together, without it triggering an icy silence or hurtful comment. I wish I could say I think Dad's a prick, and then Mom would say: *Oh no, your dad's a big sweetie.* I wish that when I tell Dad that Mom cries all the time and spends whole nights at her computer, sometimes drinking an entire bottle of wine, and when I say she often can't withdraw any money, he would then say: *That's really sad. Let me call her.* What he says instead is "I've had it with her theatrics. I'm going to do something about this. I'm sick of my children being subjected to this nonsense."

I tried to get him to help once. I told him Mom hadn't gotten out of bed for two days. "You're a drama queen just like your mother," he said. But he did send her a message afterward. I don't know what he wrote, but the following week the house had been tidied, and she was back in the kitchen making lasagna.

I can hardly finish my Big Mac, I feel so bad. I feel like a terrible child, but I know thinking like this won't help Mom. It's better to think about happy things. Like how sweet Mom is. She tickles my back every evening and lets me stay up to watch *Gossip Girl* with her. We're able to have good conversations so long as they're not about Dad. She's very open about things like sex and periods. She's a good cook and dances to hip-hop with us. No matter how sad she feels, she always lets me sleep in her bed if I want to, and she says that Luuk and I are the most important thing in her life.

Dad's sweet in different ways. Not as cuddly, but he takes Luuk to soccer matches, and he's good at explaining things I don't understand, like chemistry and politics. He often gives me money, and he's very clear about what he allows and what he doesn't. He doesn't ever stay angry for long like Mom does.

I can't help comparing the two, or wondering who I'd choose if I ever had to. But now all of a sudden there's no more choice to be made, and I'm losing my mind because we left Mom out in the cold.

In the bedroom, Laura and Dad talk in hushed voices, which reminds me of days in the past when my parents didn't want Luuk and me to hear them. He and I called it "rage whispering."

Dad says Mom has a personality disorder and that he's sure she'll turn up again. He claims she's pulled stunts like this before. Laura thinks we should call the police and warn people on Facebook.

"That's exactly what she wants."

I don't understand why he hates our mother so much. What did she ever do to him? Wasn't he the one who ran off with someone else? Or did something else happen? Why do parents always lie?

"You're talking about the mother of your children, Peter. Get a grip."

I hate Laura, but sometimes I feel sorry for her too. It seems like he's always talking about Mom.

The Grown-Up

"Stay out of this, Laura. You don't know what you're talking about."

"No, you don't know what *you're* talking about. You're so defensive you don't even see what's going on here. Whether she's crazy or not, either way, she's missing. Don't you see that by now? We need to do everything we can to find her. Before she does something crazy. Don't let yourself be blinded by your emotions."

"Me? Ha ha, that's rich. She, she's the one who's controlled by her emotions."

I hear Laura sigh. I don't understand why she stays with Dad. Mom's friend Kim doesn't either.

"He has to have a magic penis," she said to Mom the other day.

"Trust me, he doesn't."

"Anyway," Laura says now, "I'm putting the kids to bed now, and you need to make some calls. Call everyone you two were friends with. And everyone in the family. If you don't, I'll call the police."

When I was little and my parents were still together, I'd occasionally have nightmares about them divorcing and me suddenly having a different mom or dad. I'd seen kids at school go through this, and it seemed to me this was the worst thing that could happen to a person. A stranger pretending to be your mother or father, acting fake nice and fake sweet, when you know deep down: this stranger may not like me any more than I like them. They're just accepting me as part of the package because that's how it is, even though he or she would rather be alone with my mother or father. And then one day out of the blue, Laura was there.

My parents had only just separated and were still in the phase of spending time together "as friends." Back then, Mom would suddenly decide she and us kids should go out to eat with Dad, or we should all celebrate a holiday in the same house. Once, we even went on vacation together. An all-inclusive resort in Spain. Luuk and I had wanted to go there for years, for the endless buffets and water slides. It took a divorce for us to finally get what we wanted. My parents thought it was a good idea: plenty of things for the children to do, my father could play golf, my mother could read a book at the beach, and they'd put up with each other during meals.

I can still hear my mother screaming on the balcony that night, after my father decided this trip was the perfect time to tell her about Laura.

She's more than ten years younger than Dad. Laura used to work at his office but doesn't anymore now. They figured her staying on there wasn't a great idea. Of course, this had been going on for a long time already, and their months, maybe even years, of lying were the last push that sent Mom into deep despair. I think I'd do the exact opposite. I'd put up a fight and look fabulous all the time, running around town so I could rub my existence in that floozy's face every day. Mom didn't. She turned into someone who would make any man run screaming. Consumed by envy and jealousy, wallowing in contempt and moral superiority. She ended up driving away every friend but one—Kim—and put all her energy into stalling the divorce. If something like this ever happened to me, I'd give my ex the finger. I wouldn't want a single euro from him, even if it meant I had to live in a goat shed. That'll never happen anyway because I'll be making my own money no matter what. If my parents' endless fighting taught me anything, it's this: never depend on another person, either financially or emotionally.

It's happening again right now. Laura gave up her job, not him. She moved in with him and sold her house. She keeps saying she doesn't want to have her own children, but I can hear her ovaries rattling a mile away. She takes care of his kids. She's content with playing a supporting role in the hate match between my parents. Where will she go when Dad's tired of her? Because the day will come when my parents are no longer at each other's throats. What will Laura and Dad talk about then? She's seen how he operates. She'll get traded in one day too.

"I'm your bonus mom," she said to Luuk and me last Christmas. Luuk ran away from the table after she said that, and I told her she was nothing compared to our mother and we would never, ever call her that. She came and cried at the side of my bed later that night, as much as she could with that plumped-up face of hers. I hate everything about Laura. The fake way she gestures, those perfect fingernails of hers, her rock-hard eyelashes, like small spikes around her brown eyes, those eyebrows she had tattooed on. And the way she walks! Straight as an arrow, nose up, flipping back her huge hair with her little hand. She's like an Aperol Spritz-drinking doll who wears sunglasses way too big for her face. Her Instagram is one long line of selfies, in the gym or with girlfriends who all look exactly like her, and every now and then one with my father, in which he looks quite miserable.

It was never her intention to break up our family, she told me that night, sitting on my bed. She said she feels terribly guilty about it, and that she likes my mother very much and will always respect her as my primary mom.

"It's not like that," I said. "I have one mother. Not two. And I'll never have two, no matter what you call yourself."

I don't understand why a woman like Laura said something like that. It obviously was her intention to break up our family. This was the only thing on her mind for years: prying my father loose, trapping him, and luring him away with the promise that everything would be different with her. More sex, better boobs, greater love, limitless understanding, and no nagging, ever.

Only men believe such nonsense.

7.

Mom's been gone for twenty-four hours now. I use my phone to google when you can report a missing person.

> Someone you know can't be found. You don't know their whereabouts. Nearly 80% of persons reported missing turn up within 24 to 48 hours. Sometimes they're just temporarily unavailable or they've forgotten to tell others that they have an appointment. Other times, something serious has happened. What can the police do?
>
> If the police conclude that a person is not in serious danger, they will wait some time (usually 24 hours) before starting an investigation. Three-quarters of all missing persons are found within 24 hours. If the police decide the missing person is in serious danger, an investigation will be launched immediately.

I can't sleep. I creep into the hallway and sit by the stairs. I hear Dad on the phone downstairs. Most people probably won't even take his calls because they hate him. But Grandma answers.

Dad clears his throat. "Hi, Tineke. Sorry to bother you at this hour, but I was wondering if you heard from Jet today . . ."

Poor Grandma. I can picture her throwing on her coat immediately.

The Grown-Up

"No, no, relax, it's nothing serious. We have it under control here. No, you don't need to come."

Dad brings her up to speed and assures her he and Laura can handle the situation. He tells her they'll go to the police tomorrow, but he doubts the police can help in a situation like this.

"That man? No, I don't know. Do you have his name?" He listens for a minute. "Odd. I'm sure it's nothing." Silence as Grandma says something else. "Oh. I don't know how I'd be able to check that. I'm sure it's password protected. But I'm sure the police will look into it."

He thanks her and apologizes again for calling so late and worrying her. He assures her Luuk and I are fine. "I'll keep you posted. Yes, you too."

It's quiet for a long time after that, but then I hear Laura's heels. Glasses clank in the stone sink. I hear wine being poured. I picture her stroking my father's hair.

"I bet that wasn't easy."

"No." My father sighs. "No doubt Tineke is wide awake in bed now, and she'll be at our door at seven in the morning, you just wait."

"What did she say?"

"She mentioned Jet was on Tinder."

"Oh . . ."

"You can say that again. How sad."

"Well, it's quite normal these days."

Her words are dripping with sympathy. The witch.

"I don't know if I think it's normal, the mother of my children on Tinder."

"Personally, I'd be happy to see her start really living again. Isn't it good if she has someone? Then maybe she'll stop arguing with you."

"She's disappeared without a trace for the time being, Laura. It can't be that good."

"You're not jealous, are you?"

"No, I'm upset. Who knows what kind of crazy person she let into her life? Did she go out at night more times than just this?"

"Did the kids ever mention a man?"

"I don't think they know anything about this."

"And if they did, they wouldn't tell you."

Mom on Tinder. I didn't know about that. Mom often laid in bed for a long time. She'd been tired and distracted all the time recently, constantly checking her phone. Depressed, Dad said. She said it was stress. She ate very little and often went out to walk Chonk. I figured it was because she was fighting with Dad.

I return to my room, get her phone from my purse, and climb back into bed. Tinder isn't in her list of apps. I open her WhatsApp and scroll down the messages from Dad, myself, Kim, Grandma, and clients, until I come across someone she named "God." There are only two messages in the chat.

I need to talk to you, she writes. He replies with a thumbs-up, followed by: *I'll pick you up.*

I push my fist against my abdomen. When I call his number, I hear it's currently unavailable. I don't understand why Mom called someone that. I'm sure it's a joke. *Ha ha, I have a direct line to God.*

I search her contacts until I find God. There's no email or address, just the name and this cell number. Nothing unusual in her photo album either. No screenshots, no sexy selfies. I need to get into her MacBook, but it's downstairs in my backpack, which I left in the pantry.

Dad's still on the phone and Laura's puttering around in the bathroom. Couldn't I just go downstairs and say I found her Tinder date's number? That she calls him God and we need to search her MacBook for an address? Just thinking of doing this gives me goose bumps. Dad will sigh or start cursing. He'll ask what she was thinking, if she's lost her mind. I get a stomachache whenever he acts that way. Maybe I can reach Mom and convince her to come back without going through him.

I creep down the stairs.

"Yes, I know," Dad is saying. "Do you understand now?" He says something about Mom taking off for her own reasons, and what is anyone to do about that? Terrible, but he's stepped up and is taking care of me and Luuk. He thanks the person, asks them, before he hangs up, to get in touch if they hear from her.

He jumps when he sees me in the kitchen. His face is red and a little puffy. He's holding a glass of red wine, and there's an empty bottle by his computer.

"Lies, shouldn't you be in bed already?"

Dad always talks to me like I'm eight.

"You don't really think I can sleep, do you?"

Dad just looks at me.

"Why are you telling everyone Mom's some kind of depressed madwoman? You barely talk to her. You hardly even see her. What do you know about it?"

"Sweetie, I was married to your mom for quite some time. We might not get along anymore, but I know her very well."

"I don't think you do. Sometimes she's sad about you, or angry, but she's also sweet and usually in a good mood. Now you're acting like she's gone missing because she lost her mind. Or wants to commit suicide."

The last word makes him wince.

"Knowing her, she'll just turn up at the door all of a sudden tomorrow." He gives me a fake-looking smile.

I walk over and throw my arms around him. His body is trembling. He puts his hand on my head and sticks his nose in my hair. I can smell wine, Dior Homme, and a little sweat. I wish I knew if he's actually worried or just pretending for our sake.

"I know Mom can often be sweet too," he whispers.

"The first year after your divorce, she let me sleep in her bed every night. But not anymore after that." It just comes out.

"Well, you're a bit too old for that, aren't you?"

I step back right away.

"Don't you need to walk Chonk?" I say.

8.

Everyone's asleep. I'm on the toilet with Mom's phone, looking for her dating account again. I go to the App Store and type "Tinder." A cloud and arrow appear, which means she might have removed the app but kept the account. I press "download app," log in with Facebook, and voilà! Her mouth is smiling in her profile picture, but her eyes aren't. She's used a filter, which makes the image look kind of fake and a bit sad. I recognize her bedroom behind her. Her iPhone's shadow half covers her face. Her light-blue blouse is unbuttoned a bit too far, and her big curly hair is pulled back. Red lipstick makes her look like she's trying too hard. My mother, on display, reducing herself to some hot chick, when she's so much more: sweet, insecure, funny, discouraged, and upset at times. Lonely, I think. But her profile says none of this. It says:

> *I have a great job! 2 kids, with me every other week. Creative, spontaneous, sweet but sometimes intense, sensuous and beautiful, strong and soft, loves dancing and going for walks. Not desperate for a relationship but looking for warmth, friendship, and intimacy, and open to wherever that leads...*

I could have helped her, could have told her this photo won't attract the type of man she's looking for. Though I'm not entirely sure now what she's looking for. I didn't know she was looking at all. She'd said she'd had it with men. That even if she'd wanted to find one, she couldn't. Her heart was shut now, and besides, she couldn't do that to us after all we went through following the divorce and with Dad's new girlfriend. No, she was perfectly content with us and our new house, and she enjoyed her time alone during the week when we're with Dad.

Lying comes as naturally to my parents as peeing.

Her Tinder inbox has twenty-six messages. Twenty opening lines that boil down to *Hey, let's grab a drink together,* to which Mom didn't even respond. One message stands out. From a guy named Tom. Forty-seven years old and wearing a hat in his profile picture. Obviously bald. He's an entrepreneur, but then they all are. His profile reads:

Gentleman with a few rough edges, exuberant, bon vivant par excellence. Two children I unfortunately only have with me once every two weeks.

His message reads:

Hey gorgeous, your photo touches me. Something in your eyes . . . Disappointed? You're vulnerable, and that makes you beautiful and real. Funny, I'm only just on here and you're the first person I see. No need to look any further. I'd love to talk with you. Send me your number if you want to get together.

Mom answers that she thinks his profile is rather vague. And that she doesn't just give out her number. There's no reply for a full week. Then:

Sorry! I was really busy. Yeah, a vague profile. I'm only just on here but already want to leave. Too many weirdos here, not my thing. Except for you. When are we getting that drink? I'll give you my number, just text me when you're in the mood. I'm

about to get off Tinder. I'll send more pics through WhatsApp ☺
Here it is: 06-34195203.

It's not God's number. I'm sore from sitting, so I flush and go back to bed. It's 3:18. I can't stop now. There has to be more. I want to find out everything so when we go to the police, they can start searching immediately. I get her MacBook and type "Tom" in the Finder. No results. Then "God." This brings up a Word document with that title. I forward it to my own mailbox. I also find a folder that can only be opened with a password. I try Mom's birth year, but that doesn't work. Then our postal code, followed by my birth year, after which I get a notification that I've entered an incorrect password three times and the file will be locked for twenty-four hours. I'm also no longer able to email the file to myself. There's a USB drive in the drawer next to my bed, so I copy the folder to that. I check Mom's browser history and see she's searched "toxic love," "sociopaths," and "in love with a narcissist."

All of a sudden the screen grays out.

Enter your system lock to unlock this Mac.

I get her phone, hoping there's a system lock on there somewhere, but the phone's grayed out too.

This device has been locked. Contact the Apple help desk.

I google what all this means on my own phone. It appears someone's remotely hacked and wiped my mother's phone and computer. Why would anyone do this? Why would *Mom* do this?

Because she doesn't want anybody to find her.

Or because someone else doesn't want her to be found.

9.

White tiles. A toilet. I try to move, but my body's paralyzed, just like in a dream. I can barely open my eyes, and my tongue is so swollen I can hardly breathe. *Get up, goddammit!* My head feels separate from my arms and legs, which are heavy.

I'm in a bathroom. Not mine.

On and off, I feel a pang of fear, but then the feeling subsides, along with the energy it gives me. I'm afraid I'll never see my children again, and the thought restores my will to fight.

The car on the bumpy path. God suddenly collapsing in my lap, crying. His hands on my hips. Snippets of memory, not in any chronological order. Another one: him sitting on the bed. There's wine. He tells me I have serious problems. "You're incapable of emotional attachment." His voice, his opinion. He sounds insistent. "I only want to treat you right. I could make you so happy if you'd only let me, dammit."

We have pornographic sex. He says it's the best sex he's ever had. I'm watching us from a distance. He's pulling my hair. I don't feel anything. No pain, no revulsion, no pleasure. I'm like a machine, doing what I've been programmed to do. I moan when I'm supposed to. "You like that, don't you?" I'm not in my body anymore.

He tries to work himself into me. "I want all of you."

I need to go home.

"What would it take for this to stop?" I choose my words carefully. We're in the car. I need to convince him to drive us back to civilization. "Could you please take me home?"

He starts the car. I'm breathing more easily now. He lets out a sharp laugh.

"Let's discuss this like grown-ups. I love you, Jet, and I know I've been going about this all wrong. Please let me explain."

"I want to go home. My children are alone."

"Lies is seventeen. She can babysit just fine."

"I forgot my phone. She can't reach me."

"She has a father too. Knock it off. I'll take you home later. You had no problem leaving them home before."

There haven't been that many other times. I went to see him once before while Lies and Luuk were at home, sleeping. And I felt really bad about it.

"I can see it in those eyes: you don't love me anymore. Not like I love you. And I want a thousand percent. I want it all. That's just how I am. You don't. You're scared."

He drives in the direction of the little vacation house. "Come on. Just one drink. You can at least give me a proper goodbye. It's very close."

I only wanted someone who would touch me. Someone who cared about me in a different way from my kids, my friends, my mother. It's so lonely, the long nights, waking up and eating in front of the television. I wanted more than that. But here I am, lying on a tiled floor, and the only thing that seems to be working still is my brain.

I take in small breaths, conserving my energy.

He helps me into the bath. He gently, attentively works his way across my body with a washcloth. He washes my hair, scrubs my nails. I'm not sure if this is real or a dream. I've surrendered. That's how he likes to see me: broken. It doesn't matter. It's what I deserve. I went out looking, took the risk. I should have known better.

The Grown-Up

Suddenly his face looms above me. A pitying look, no more anger. I'm lying in a bed. I've slept apparently, but I don't know for how long. I can move my limbs again.

"Hey, pretty thing." He acts like nothing happened.

My head is pounding. There's a painful bump on my left temple.

"That didn't go quite as planned, did it?" He chuckles and sits down beside me. I can smell his shower gel and deodorant. He gently runs his hand through my hair, then hands me a glass of Coke.

"Drink it slowly—it helps with nausea."

"What the hell happened?"

"You were a bit sick. From the wine, I think."

"I don't remember anything. Bits and pieces. I thought you were going to kill me."

"I was so upset, I nearly could have." He laughs again, his teeth shining bright. The beautiful God is back.

I sit up and try to remember anything about last night. I know we talked and drank wine. I know I was about to end things with him. I try to access the memories that must be stored in my head, but I can't.

"How did I get this?" I touch the bruise and can feel a scab.

"You fell. In the bathroom. You were completely hammered. You wouldn't let me even get close. You threw up everywhere. I was mopping all night and had to change the sheets twice. Any pain?"

I nod.

"Would you like some Tylenol?"

"I want to go home."

He gets a bottle of tablets from the drawer beside his bed and hands me two. "A thousand milligrams works best."

I take the over-the-counter meds with some water. "Why didn't you take me home? My children are all alone. I want to talk to them. Can I use your phone?"

"Will you stop already?" His expression looks ominous. It hits me then. He's lying. Those pills weren't over-the-counter painkillers. My dream wasn't a dream.

"Please, take me home, or call a taxi. I won't tell anyone about this."

He sits down beside me and strokes my cheek. "About what?"

"About you kidnapping me."

He lets out a roaring laugh. "All right, Sticks, we'll leave pretty soon. I promise."

"No, now. Or I'll run out of the house and start screaming."

"Good luck with that. Feel free. Run outside, scream as loud as you want. Go on, then!" He pokes me.

I get up, wobbling as if I'm drunk. There's no time to grab my clothes. Every second counts. I stumble as the hallway spins all around. I have to keep my wits about me. When I try the front door, it's locked. I turn around. God is laughing in the bedroom doorway.

"Oh, you should see yourself!"

The patio door. I grab the side table and lift it above my head. I stumble for a moment, then with my last ounce of strength heave the table through the glass door, which shatters into thousands of little pieces.

10.

My bladder is burning. I walk to the bathroom holding my fist against my abdomen. The light's on already, and the door is locked. "Just a second!" Laura says.

I run downstairs. Luuk's on the sofa in front of the TV, his headphones on. I go into the other bathroom and finally relieve myself. There's a drop of blood.

Mom, I think, staring at the birthday calendar on the door. *Where are you?*

Dad walks in the front door and shouts at Chonk, who's scuffing up the perfect white floor. "It's alright!" I hear Laura call out in a high voice. I want to go home, our old home. I want Laura to have gone missing and for no one to care. I want to walk in the kitchen and see Mom and Dad laughing like they used to. They've forgotten, but they used to laugh a lot. They had sex too. I saw them one night. They were sitting in the middle of the living room fully naked, my mother on top of my father. I like to remember that they loved each other once. Only, when I remind them, they both look horrified.

"When are we going to the police?" I ask.

Dad's making coffee. Laura sits at the kitchen island in her floral robe while Luuk sullenly eats a grilled peanut butter sandwich.

"In a little while," Dad says.

"Have you learned anything?" Laura asks. Dad shakes his head. We're all startled by the doorbell moments later. Chonk runs out of the pantry, barking.

"Oh my God," Laura says and puts her hand on her chest.

"Calm down, it's Grandma," Dad says to Chonk. He buzzes Grandma in using the intercom.

When she walks in, Luuk throws himself into her arms like he hasn't seen her in years.

"Oh, dear children." Grandma's chin trembles. I nearly cry but bite my cheek to stop myself.

Dad extends a hand. "Hi, Tineke."

"Don't be silly, Peter," Grandma says and gives him a kiss. "And you must be Laura."

Laura nods and shakes her hand. I see Grandma's nose briefly twitch, as if detecting a foul odor.

"I was awake all night, you guys. This is quite a mess. Peter, have you learned anything new? Did you inform the police?"

"Sorry, no. We actually wanted to do that after breakfast."

I need to pee again, but I don't go. It's so good that Grandma's here. A bit of Mom at least, someone who loves her just as much as Luuk and I do. Someone who'll finally do something, because Grandma sticks her nose into everything. That's why Dad doesn't like her.

"One thing is certain. Your mother would never leave you two alone this long without a reason. Something must have happened."

"If you're here to upset everyone—"

Grandma raises her hand and cuts Dad off. "I'm here to look for my daughter, the mother of your children. Not to bicker."

"This doesn't seem like the time to jump to conclusions, especially in front of the kids."

"Your children are frightened, Peter. If we shut them out, they'll only become more frightened. Plus, they know her best, don't you guys?"

Luuk and I nod.

The Grown-Up

Now that Grandma's here, I have the nerve to say it. "I have her phone and MacBook, but I think someone did a remote wipe last night." I don't mention I was able to save two files.

Everyone's silent for a moment. Grandma gives me a serious look.

"Does anyone want any coffee?" Laura asks.

"Please. What does this mean, Peter? Sorry, I'm a bit behind the times."

"You can lock or erase your devices only if you also have the password and Apple ID. So maybe . . . she did this herself?"

"Or she was hacked," Laura says.

"Hacked?"

"They break into your iCloud, or into your computer."

"Why would they do that?"

"To cover tracks," I say.

"Why would Mom want to cover her tracks?" Luuk asks.

"Or someone else . . . ," I say.

"It won't be to take her money," Dad mumbles.

"No," Grandma says. "You already took care of that."

I can't hold it any longer and say I have to pee. Luuk asks if he can play his game until we go to the police.

"You don't have to come. You can stay here with Laura," Dad says.

Luuk angrily shakes his head. I take a glass with me into the bathroom upstairs and use it to catch my pee. I hold the glass to the light: it's cloudy. I need to see a doctor. I look for painkillers in the drawer under the sink and find Laura's Lactacyd Refreshing Intimate Tissues. Would those help against a bladder infection? I put them in the pocket of my bathrobe and take two Tylenol, then pocket the bottle.

11.

"Look, a whole family," the police officer says. He's rather handsome and doesn't seem much older than me. He's a ginger, like Prince Harry. "My name's Jochem." We introduce ourselves and follow Jochem into a windowless room that smells of stale cigarettes and Clorox.

"My daughter didn't come home last night," Grandma starts, and I immediately add that the missing woman is my mother. "And my ex-wife," Dad says. Luuk doesn't say anything. He takes my hand and presses his nose against my sleeve.

"How awful. I'll just go get two extra chairs. Do any of you want coffee?"

Jochem gives me a long look. I shake Luuk off of me. He sees a child, of course. I should have worn something else. But you can hardly wear your Sunday best when your mother's just gone missing.

"Please," I say.

When we entered the main hall a moment ago, I saw posters on the wall. Faces of people the police are looking for. Most looked very frightening, criminals I suspect, but there were children too. Would they hang my mother beside them?

We give Jochem as many details about Mom's disappearance as we can. There aren't that many. She has long, curly blond hair, a whole lot of it, and usually wears it pulled back. Blue eyes, slim build, no tattoos. She usually wears jeans, boots, and a gray or camel-colored sweater. Neither Luuk nor I knows if this is what she was wearing the

The Grown-Up

other night, and I feel guilty about this immediately. Funny how you don't really pay attention when you're just living. Mom's just there, and whether or not she's happy, what she's wearing, even what she's saying isn't something we really think about.

"She took us up to bed, like always," Luuk says. "We talked about school a bit, and how I had to clean my room."

"She took a bath afterward," I say. I remember all of a sudden. "And I heard her talking."

"Do you know who she was talking to?"

"No."

"Maybe she was on the phone with someone," Grandma says.

Dad uneasily shifts around in his chair.

"I found out her MacBook was wiped," I say. "Someone did that last night, remotely."

"She could have done that herself," Jochem says.

"Why would she?"

"That's what we'll try to find out. We'll need a recent picture of her."

I offer to send him one from my phone. "Do you want her MacBook and phone too?" I ask.

"Is there a reason to assume your mother is in immediate danger?"

"She has to be. Mom would never just leave us alone without saying anything," I say.

"She does go out and walk the dog," Luuk adds.

"Sure, for ten minutes at a time. Or she'll have dinner with a friend, but then she leaves me in charge. We're not babies anymore."

"Would you mind if I had a word alone with your father and grandmother for a moment?"

"No," Luuk says.

"I know the most about her," I say. "Mom tells me everything. So maybe you should also have a word alone with me."

"Good idea," Jochem says. "We'll do that afterward, okay?"

Luuk and I are pushed off on a woman who talks ridiculously loud and childishly. She calls me "milady" and Luuk "good sir." But I'm no child. I'm seventeen. I've already French-kissed a boy. I know exactly what's going on here. We had to leave so Dad and Grandma could speak freely about Mom's mental state. Dad'll say she was depressed and slept a lot, and Grandma will snap that that's because of Dad and his "child bride." Dad will then insist she shouldn't close her eyes to her own share of the blame, after which Jochem will no doubt conclude that Mom's left to get a break from them and will come back on her own when she's good and ready. This whole episode will be used by Dad's lawyers to take us away from Mom.

I ask where the bathroom is. It feels like my bladder is filled with hydrochloric acid. I need antibiotics, but before the doctor gives them to me she'll take a swab and ask if I'm wiping from front to back and if I'm drinking enough cranberry juice. The pain is always there, I'll say. She'll answer that the infection might be caused by the divorce. In other words, by my anxiety. Like that's supposed to help me. Ever since hearing that a classmate of mine had to have a procedure to stretch her urethra so she'd stop getting UTIs, I've been afraid to see a doctor at all.

"Are you alright?" Grandma asks from behind the bathroom door.

"Sure," I say. This toilet smells like piss. Surely countless gallons have been peed here by countless nervous people. Someone has scratched *fuck the police* on the door.

"You've been in there an awful long time . . . The officer wants to have a word with you too, Lies."

"I'm coming out now."

"Is your bladder acting up again?"

"A bit."

"Oh, darn it."

I love Grandma, even if she can be terribly annoying. She's actually the only one who really looks out for us, and sometimes she sees things my parents don't. Like how Luuk is something of a video game addict, for instance. And when I'm in pain, she knows. I can't lie to her. If I did, she'd know right away.

The Grown-Up

I think Jochem's quite handsome. I hardly dare look at him. I sometimes think I might like older men, but I don't want to end up like Laura, with a man who's been through it all already and constantly complains about his ex-wife.

"You were talking about a man on Tinder and your mother's computer and phone. Were you by any chance able to find out his details?" Jochem sits opposite me behind a laptop.

"Sorry, no. Well, that his name's Tom and that he's wearing a hat in his profile picture. He has two kids and he's an entrepreneur."

"Do you have any screenshots?"

"No." Silly I didn't think of that.

"And why do you think this man has something to do with your mother's disappearance?"

I shrug. "It's the only unusual thing I found. Oh, and a message in the neighborhood watch WhatsApp group. The neighbors said something about a black VW Golf. They also shared a screenshot of the license plate. Apparently this car was parked in the middle of the street for quite some time."

"Do you know this car?"

"Nope."

"Do you have the license plate for me?"

"44-XB-UW."

"Thanks, we'll run it through. Do you have your mother's computer and phone with you?"

I get my bag and put the devices on the table. "But like I said already, there's nothing on them anymore."

Jochem diligently writes everything down. "Would you happen to know her login?"

"As far as I know, her password is always Chonk2017. Are you going to look for her now? Or how does this work from here?"

"I write everything down, and then I pass this on to my colleagues from criminal investigations, who'll get to work on it. But I'd recommend you keep asking around: on Facebook and Twitter, in the neighborhood. Your father said she's gone missing for a few days before."

He can be such a jerk.

"Like when?" I ask.

"About a year ago. After an argument about his new girlfriend."

I dig deep into my memory. They argued about Laura nearly every week, and Mom walked away from him furious every time. But she always came back home.

"She was in a hotel for a few days?" Jochem says.

"Oh, but that was because our old house was being renovated. Something in the kitchen. She had to get the house ready to sell."

"And you don't think she's just taking a break somewhere? Maybe she's really angry with your father and this is her way of dealing with it?"

I put my hands deeper into my pockets and squeeze the skin of my stomach hard. "That's what Dad always says, but he doesn't know her like I do. Mom says so too: 'We don't know each other anymore. We've become strangers.' She would never leave us alone this long without us knowing where she is. Even if she did leave, Luuk and I would be able to reach her. She would always have left a note. And she's not depressed. She's sad sometimes or angry, and sometimes really tired. But that's not so strange since she just moved and has to work and take care of us."

Jochem gives me a serious look. He feels sorry for me, obviously. *These poor children,* I see him think, just like all my teachers. *This poor girl with those terrible parents.* I don't want everyone to think my parents are terrible, so I don't say anything about them anymore.

"You know most missing persons are found alive and well within twenty-four to forty-eight hours?" he says.

"Yes. I have Google."

"Anything else we need to know?"

"She would never abandon us. Someone has her."

Jochem presses his lips together. "Has your father ever been violent?"

The Grown-Up

I'm afraid to look him in the eye. "No. They've argued a lot. He might have pushed her once, but not like you think."

"What am I thinking?"

"That he could seriously harm her."

"It can also be an accident sometimes."

They'd already broken up, but Luuk and I were happy to see them talking in the kitchen of our old home as if they still liked each other. It was like old times. We were in front of the television, eating the chips Mom gave us. It was clear she didn't want Luuk and me to bother them. She had rosy cheeks, and she was constantly twirling her hair. They were drinking wine, and Mom had something yummy in the oven. I now think she wanted to lure him back with the smell of garlic and chicken, us two kids clean and sweet on the sofa, her in that dress she wore only on special occasions. All of a sudden, we heard a chair fall over. Mom screamed.

"Get a grip, Jet," Dad said.

We went to the kitchen. Mom was hitting him, crying.

"The kids," Dad said.

"They already know what an asshole you are."

"Why don't you guys go upstairs for a little while," Dad said.

Luuk hung on to me and started to cry.

"Out of my house!" Mom was screeching now.

"It's still my house too," Dad said.

"You ran out on us. Nothing here belongs to you anymore, do you hear me?"

"Ha! Just a moment ago you said, 'This is your home too, Peter.'" He imitated her voice.

Mom's face was covered in tears and snot. She went at him again, but this time Dad saw it coming. He grabbed her by the wrists and pressed her against the wall. "Will you stop? Will you stop now?"

Mom bit his arm.

"Dad, you need to leave." I said it as calmly as I could, grabbing his hand. "Let Mom go."

His eyes were teary too. He released her and waved his finger in front of her face. "It's unacceptable, Jet, this kind of drama. I'm never coming here again. You'll get the paperwork in the mail this week."

He gave Luuk and me each a kiss and a pat, and then he got out of there. Luuk was crying. Mom collapsed on the floor, and we huddled against her.

"Why'd you do that, Mom?" Luuk sobbed. "Why were you fighting? Now he's gone forever."

12.

"This child has a bladder infection. We just need a prescription," Grandma says to the medical center's receptionist.

"You'll still have to wait for the doctor." The receptionist puts a plastic cup on the counter, applies a sticker with my name on it, and asks me to go pee in it.

Grandma tells her that I have them all the time, says that we shouldn't have to go through all that when we know what the problem is. I can tell from the look in the receptionist's eyes she thinks Grandma's an overbearing nag.

"Never mind, Grandma. Let's not argue." I don't understand why grown-ups think being angry will change someone else's mind. It's always the opposite. Just look at Mom and Dad.

In the packed waiting room, Grandma feels my cheeks. "Do you have a fever?" Her hands are trembling.

"I don't think so."

"The police will find her. They're so good these days. I thought he was a very nice fellow, that Jochem." She's rambling now. "That man she was dating, did she tell you about him?"

"No."

"She didn't tell me much either. I got the idea it hadn't worked out. Your mother's a bit cagey, isn't she? Doesn't share anything. Not like you, dearie. But why wouldn't she?"

I rest my head against her soft arm. The other people in the waiting room stare at their phones.

"You don't ever need to feel ashamed about anything, Lies."

I have plenty to feel ashamed about. Starting with the fact that we're sitting here and not outside looking for her. Every minute could be crucial.

"She'll pop up again all of a sudden, you'll see. I can feel it. I think you can really feel it when something's wrong, don't you think? Every mother is connected to her child by thousands of invisible threads. Her and me, her and you. You'll see. She's an adult, with a good brain . . ." The more Grandma says, the less convinced I am everything will be alright.

I go back to the bathroom to pee. The pain is getting worse, and spreading. It was behind my pubic bone, but now it's shooting up my back, and there's a ball of fire throbbing in my gut. I get out my phone, open Facebook, and type a message.

> My mother, Jet Verschoor, 45 years old, left our house at night two days ago and has been missing ever since. She was probably wearing jeans, a camel-colored sweater, and yellow patent leather boots. We miss her terribly and are worried. Does anyone know something, or did anyone see her somewhere? If so, please call the police, or me. A DM via FB is alright too. Please share this message on all your social media.

I include my phone number and that of the police, along with a good, recent picture of Mom. Afterward, I take a screenshot and share the message on Instagram. I try not to look at the photo for too long.

"Yep, we're looking at a urinary tract infection, alright. Her urine is chock-full of leukocytes—that is, white blood cells. I'll write a prescription." She turns to me. "Do you drink cranberry juice?"

I drink it all. Bearberry tea, cranberry juice, goldenrod.

"Nothing helps," Grandma says.

"Then maybe it's time to go see a urologist." The doctor types out the prescription on the computer. I can feel futile tears burning and I squeeze my thumbs between my fingers.

"Her mother always had this too."

"Has," I say.

"Oh, still? See, there's something I don't know."

I think about how Mom always says: "Don't tell Grandma. She'll only start meddling, like usual."

In the car, I check my phone. There isn't a single lead among the concerned responses, but tens of people have shared my message. I open Mom's Facebook account and post it on her wall too.

Dad's calling. "Well, Lies. I see you're not waiting this out. My phone's ringing nonstop. Couldn't you have coordinated this with me first?" His voice is hoarse, like he's just been crying. "It's so real all of a sudden."

"The police officer told me to do this. You have to share it too."

He's silent for a long time. Then he says: "I did. And so did Laura. Are you coming home now?"

I don't want to go to his house. I want to go back in time.

"Do you feel terrible, Dad?"

"No, why?"

"Why aren't you upset that she's missing? You used to love Mom, didn't you?"

"Oh, you mean about that. Of course, sweetie. But it'll be alright. We'll find her."

"Will you two stop fighting then?"

"I'll do my best."

"You won't take us away from her?"

He snuffles. "Oh, sweetie . . ."

Grandma puts her hand on my leg. She's crying.

"Just come home," Dad says. "Luuk's been asking what's keeping you two all this time."

"I have a bladder infection, by the way."

"I'll make tea, and Laura will make you a hot water bottle. I love you, Lies."

"Love you, Dad."

Grandma and I exchange a glance. She seems to want to say something but then apparently decides it's best to keep her mouth shut.

13.

It's dark again. I'm in bed, a hot water bottle on my stomach. The antibiotics must be starting to kick in, because I'm feeling nauseous. The rain pelts against the windows. I hope that Mom's inside somewhere and that she isn't alone. She can't handle being alone too well, and every time I'm in this room in my dad's house, in this bed, I think about that. Mom home alone on the sofa. She doesn't cook when we're gone; she just eats a bag of chips in front of the television, hunkered down until we come home again. It annoys Dad when I message her a lot, so I count the days until I can go back. *Only six, five, four more nights.*

I hear Laura and my father laughing downstairs. How can they do that? In this strange, unsightly, inhospitable place, it feels like the past has been erased. It's only a matter of time until Laura has a baby, Mom says. Just wait. Then the whole thing will start all over again, and Luuk and I will be replaced once and for all.

I've added Tom's and God's numbers in my phone. Neither of them answer when I call. I message them on WhatsApp.

> Hi, I found your number on my mother's phone. Could you call me back? It's about my mother. Best regards, Lies

I stare at the message. Should I also write something about her having gone missing? No. The less information they have, the better.

Though obviously they'll already know if they're friends on Facebook. My phone rings, a number I don't recognize. I answer.

"This is Tom."

I hear him taking in air and letting it out. One of those heavy breathers. It sounds disgusting. I tell Tom Mom's been missing for two days and nights and ask if he's seen or heard from her.

"I only went on one date with your mother."

I quickly try to think of things to ask him. "Umm, when was this?"

"Oh dear, that was months ago already. We went for coffee at a bar. Festina Lente, I think. We had a good time, but that's as far as it went."

"So you weren't seeing each other?"

"We messaged back and forth a bit. But I got the feeling she wasn't really interested in me. I believe there was someone else."

"Do you maybe know who this other person was?"

"No. She didn't explicitly say there was somebody, but she didn't want to meet up anymore. I wasn't under the impression she was seriously looking for a new relationship. She got on Tinder because everyone around her was saying she had to move on. At least, that's what she said."

"Why do you think there was someone else?"

"She changed her WhatsApp profile picture. That's what women do when they like someone. At first, she had a photo with her dog, then all of a sudden some sexy selfie. I wrote her a message to compliment her for the nice photo, but she never replied."

I wonder if I should believe him. As if a man would ever say, *Now that you ask, yes, I've been stalking her for months already, and I locked her up in a cellar the night before yesterday.* Either way, he was keeping an eye on her profile pictures and had made his own story out of it changing.

"What kind of car do you drive?"

"A burgundy Kia Niro."

"'Gentleman with a few rough edges . . .'"

Tom lets out a muffled laugh. "Terrible, isn't it? I was on Tinder only a week and only dated your mother."

The Grown-Up

I don't believe him. His profile was much too slick for someone who doesn't like online dating. "I'm curious what those rough edges are."

"How old are you?"

"Seventeen."

"You're quite sassy for such a young girl."

I don't like him. I don't think my mother did either. But then why did she agree to meet him?

"Your mother spoke highly of you two."

I want to bury myself under my comforter and never wake up. The idea of my mother going to a bar with a loser like this and talking about us makes me want to puke.

Everything fell apart when my parents started letting strangers into our family.

Laura has cooked, but none of us have any appetite, especially for vegetarian cordon bleu. "It really does taste just like meat," she says curtly when Luuk makes retching noises. I only take a bite of broccoli. Laura's cheeks are shaking from stress. She asks Dad if he can just put his phone down for five minutes. One of them must have thought it would be nice for us to sit at the kitchen island together, but the stools are too tall, the lights too bright, the black stone counter too cold.

"No one heard or saw anything," Dad says, and for a moment I think I hear genuine concern in his voice. I look up from my plate. He still cares about Mom after all. Laura's jaws are working frantically. She always moves like some part of her body is stiff, and when she kisses you her cheekbones bump against yours a bit too hard. *Can't imagine her being good in bed,* Evi said the other day. Why couldn't Laura be the one who disappeared?

"It looks like Mom planned her departure very well," Dad says. He might as well have slapped us, the words hit so hard.

"What's that supposed to mean?" I say. Luuk spits all the broccoli back onto his plate.

"For God's sake, Peter, don't be an idiot," Laura hisses.

"Calm down, guys. I only meant that no one knows anything, no one noticed anything about her, no one saw her, and she's erased all her tracks."

"Why do you assume she erased them?" I say. "You act like she wanted to disappear. I'm sure that's not the case. Someone has her."

"Well then who, Lies? I've spoken to all her contacts. Even a few of her patients."

"Clients," I say. "And everyone's entitled to have secrets, aren't they? Have you ever considered the possibility that she doesn't want to share hers with you?"

"Lies, I'd say a person forfeits their right to privacy when they go missing, wouldn't you?"

"Don't act like such a lawyer, Peter," says Laura, seizing the opportunity to make herself more popular with Luuk and me.

"Listen, kids, I was with Mom for twenty years. I know her. I know how private she is, and also how sensitive. Extremely happy sometimes, depressed at others. That's when she starts making things up. I really think that she just wants a bit of peace and quiet and that she'll show up suddenly with some explanation. Every now and then, she'd say how she felt like just getting on a train and heading south. And now she's done it."

"Without any money, without a phone, without her kids," I say.

"She knows you're in good hands with us, and she knew you had access to money, and that you had phones. I know this theory hurts, guys, but it's the most plausible explanation. Because why would anyone kidnap Mom?"

"Because they're out of their mind? Doesn't she work with people like that?" Laura downs the rest of her white wine in one gulp.

"She doesn't work with the criminally insane, Laura. She works with housewives who suffer nervous breakdowns and men with midlife crises."

"Both of those can get pretty crazy too, you know?"

"She was in love," I bluff. Luuk leaves the table and runs upstairs.

"Let me handle it," Laura says and runs after him.

"Why didn't you tell us that before?" Dad asks.

I shrug. I can tell from the way he's squinting that my words hit their mark.

"With who?"

"I don't know. Some guy called Tom. I have his number."

"My God, Lies, you're just like her. You need to give that number to the police."

"I did that already. Obviously." I walk away from the kitchen island, following Luuk and Laura.

They think I'm in bed, but I'm on the toilet with my glass of water and my phone. The painful peeing is over and now I've got diarrhea from the antibiotics. *If there is a God, then he hates women,* Mom always says. *Because he gave us just enough ailments to keep us stuck behind men for all eternity.*

Dad and Laura are in their bathroom, brushing their teeth, when all of a sudden she screams: "Will you please just once shut up about her? You left her two years ago, goddammit, but you act like it was yesterday. She was dating, isn't that great? What do you want if not that? For her to spend her whole life crying and waiting for you? What the fuck is wrong with you men?"

If Mom had wanted to drive Dad and Laura apart by disappearing, then she's nearly succeeded. *You can come back now, Mom. She's not going to make it.*

"What do you know about it? I'm serious, Laura, you don't know anything! Do you have any idea how terrible I feel? What I left behind for you?"

"For me? For *me?*"

"That's right, for you."

"So now it's all my fault?"

Dad mumbles something, and then I hear him walk away like he used to do with Mom whenever things got too complicated—right into the arms of someone who supposedly understood him better. Laura cries now like Mom used to cry, and even though I hate her I also feel sorry for her. *Know what you're getting into, girl,* Mom said to her once when they'd all decided it was in our best interests for them to get along. I suspect Laura knows now.

When all is quiet in the house, I go back to bed and flip open my MacBook. I'm nervous as hell because I'm about to enter her secret world again. At the same time, I feel terrible about snooping. Chonk lies beside me on the bed even though Dad doesn't want him to. I try to open the Word document titled GOD that I emailed to myself, but it seems to be password-protected. I try her default password, Chonk2017. Nothing. I type the acronym she assigned to her therapy model: RAAR. *Recognize, Acknowledge, Accept, Release.* RAAR2017. Wrong. 2018, 2019, and 2020 don't work either. I type my name, then Luuk's; our old address, new address, places of birth; Dad's family name, hers; the name of our cat who passed away, and then I do the same with GOD. GOD2018. GOD2019. GOD1234. Gotcha.

It was the second day of Christmas, and I'd dropped my kids off at Peter's new place. I left them there down by the entrance, each with a backpack. It was raining and windy, and the streets were empty except for us. The kids begged me to please come upstairs with them. I tried to hold back my tears. "You're going to have a great time with Dad."

I couldn't go in there, into that shiny hallway with all the brass plates, tropical plants, and tall windows in black steel frames. I could feel the anger pounding in my belly, a feeling that would surely break loose if I saw him, or her, in their fancy apartment. The life that was taken from me. My children, with that other woman for a whole week. Their Christmas tree, her family. Who asked for this? I didn't. The children sure didn't. The two of them with a stranger, me alone in that deteriorating house, which was for sale at the time. I'd helped many others get through this process, but only now did I understand what it meant to feel completely superfluous and alone.

The first thing I did when I got home was tear down the Christmas tree. I dragged it through the room, screaming, throwing and smashing ornaments, stomping on the tree topper. After that I went at the chair, the one he always sat in next to the fireplace but that he didn't want to take to his new apartment because it didn't match what he called "our style." I lunged at it with a kitchen knife until I was exhausted, my anger spent.

Do I really want to know all this about Mom? Why did she write this down? Because she was falling apart, probably, like I am now. I think back to that Christmas, the most godawful Christmas in my entire life. We'd just gotten used to the fact that Mom and Dad were separated. Dad had been living in an apartment in the Rivers neighborhood, which Mom referred to as a typical divorced man's pad, for nearly a year. It had a sofa, a bed, a ridiculously large TV, and a starter set of Ikea furniture. Dad couldn't have us there very often, so we went out to eat or to the movies with him once in a while.

At our old house, we lived closely with Mom, the three of us sleeping and eating, laughing and crying, cooking, walking, bickering the same way old married couples do. Mom was sad, it's true, but also determined to make this work for us. Once the divorce was settled and Dad had bought and renovated his apartment—"Finally I can set up my own place just the way I want it!"—the parenting plan took effect. Joint custody. *As if he was ever a coparent during our marriage,* I heard Mom say to Kim. But it had been agreed in court, so there we went with our backpacks.

I'd vowed to push through the pain. Kim would message me, Mom would call, but at first I didn't reply. They kept messaging and calling until I told them I was fine but I needed to be alone. I wasn't able to share this grief, and I felt ashamed of the mess Peter and I had made. Of how I'd essentially left my children at a stranger's doorstep. (Sure, Peter's their father, but he had turned into a stranger at the other end of the table, with the help of another stranger.) I was ashamed of how I spoke ill of him to the kids. How I'd fly at him right in front of them. How I'd become consumed by anger. Ashamed of my loneliness and my lack of energy to move beyond it. It'll pass, I hear my mother say. My father hanged himself, so she knows how it feels to be abandoned. I understood my dad now. Incapable of picturing a future. Feeling wholly superfluous and worthless, down at the bottom of a black well, so deep no light can ever enter. You're willing to act like there's a way out, only you're too tired to find it. The only reason I'm not dead is because I wouldn't do that to my kids. That's what I was thinking that afternoon, that evening.

Still, I tidied everything up again, took the chair and Christmas tree to the backyard, vacuumed the room with the radio tuned to the Top 40. I went to Albert Heijn for groceries dressed in Lies's gray tracksuit, smelling of her perfume. A basketful of Casa di Mama pizzas, a bottle of white wine, and Christmas chocolates. Boozing with Netflix, and only six nights to go before they'd be home again.

Last Christmas, Luuk and I had dinner at Dad and Laura's apartment. The Loft, they call it, like it's New York. Together with Grandpa and Grandma, plus Laura's parents, who are a bit basic and were so impressed they didn't know what to say. From the lowly city of Roermond to Amsterdam's posh Zuidas district: hats off to their little Laura once again. You can no longer tell from Laura's accent that she's originally from Limburg, but her parents were hard to understand. By the time Luuk and I had retreated to the sofa in front of the giant TV to watch *Stranger Things,* Laura had already had a bit too much wine. In that piercing voice of hers, she announced that though she might not have given birth to any children herself, at least her parents already were a grandpa and grandma of sorts. Her father's muttering was drowned out by the sound of our actual, rather posh grandpa. "I rather think that title should be reserved for blood relations." Laura has an amazing talent for making herself unpopular in a split second.

It's as if Mom's on the bed with me and talking to me, only now I'm not her child but a girlfriend, a grown-up, someone she takes seriously. We laugh about my Christmas story together. *That darn Laura*. I recognize in myself the same desire Mom felt to break something, the anger surging and settling onto my shoulders like a yoke.

That's why I'm writing all this down. Better to write than to tear the house apart, or to damage my kids with my sobbing. I need to pick myself up and move on. I tell my clients every day: Recognize, Acknowledge, Accept, and Release. RAAR. Use the weeks you're without them to heal yourself. I'm talking to myself now like I'm my own therapist.

I got a dog to keep active, to care for and cherish, a warm body in the house. Yes, also to forge an even closer bond with my children. Peter's going to hate me, I thought. A dog. They've been wanting one for years.

At some point that week I created a Tinder profile. Kim had been insisting on it for ages. Start dating, Jet, if only to feel like a woman again and to take your mind off Peter and that whore. That's what we call her, even if it's obviously unfair to blame her for everything. It feels good to say it, to compress all those spiteful feelings into a single word. Whore. All things considered, we should feel sorry for her. Poor child, what has she gotten herself into by walking into a family like this, with kids that'll hate her until the end of time and a man who'll eventually cheat on her too? Lying is in Peter's genes, and he'll never change. Women will keep coming and going because he's addicted to attention, to adventure, to testing the limits. I was never the only one, and Laura won't be either. Of course, he swears that he's changed, that she's everything he needs, that his unfaithful tendencies had to do with the unhappy marriage he was trying to escape. She doesn't want to hear the truth: that our marriage really wasn't that unhappy, that he'd already been cheating while we were still madly in love because it's a form of obsessive compulsion, like doing coke or counting paving stones. I warned her. She promptly blocked me.

I'd actually stopped worrying about Peter's little adventures. Things worked between us so long as he kept them far from me and he and I could pretend that side of him didn't exist. We had a kind of unspoken contract. Screwing okay, but no walking on the beach holding hands. But of course Peter couldn't keep himself from breaking the agreement. At the end of the day, screwing somebody else with your partner's permission isn't all that exciting. The real thrill lies in secrecy, so he started to have affairs. He preferred to do it within our postcode area, liked it even more with women I was close with. Forbidden love, the romance of secrets. That's how he drew in Laura, the classic office secretary. Before her, there was something with the upstairs neighbor, a teacher from school, Lies's best friend's mom, his best friend's wife. He'd have slept with Kim too, if it was up to him. So why did he leave me for Laura in the end? Because she adored him so much it was ridiculous. "I need someone who'll go for me a thousand percent," he said. It was the only time he spoke the truth.

Hadn't I gone for him a thousand percent? In the first years, of course I had. My love for him made me fade away myself. He was the successful young lawyer who'd noticed me, a chaotic, vocationally trained girl. More than that: he lavished attention on me. Even my friends felt it was a bit much at times. He'd say things like "We're not soulmates, we're one soul." There was even something romantic about him confessing his escapades, which he always did in tears, and with such regret and self-loathing, it was as if he'd had no choice in the matter and had only satisfied the woman out of the goodness of his heart. I tried to comfort him in the beginning. "Poor thing, I won't leave you all alone anymore." He had a strong sex drive, so it was best never to deny him. I had to save him from himself. In return, I thought, he would make me happier than I'd ever been. I deserved that. But what was he doing to deserve such a sweet, strong girl? Finally I asked him this, and I asked again and again, until I no longer had the energy to say it. "You can't keep looking to me for your *personal validation,"* I said then, "because I don't have the bandwidth for that anymore." *By that time, we'd had two children, and I'd gone into business for myself.*

It's a quarter to two, and I still haven't read a word about God. My eyes are burning from fatigue, but my brain's firing on all cylinders. Dad cheated with Evi's mom? Oh my God. And which teacher at school? I want to be with Mom so bad right now my whole body aches. *Where the hell are you? I understand you now that I've read this. How did you manage, all those years, with all those secrets? Always putting dinner on the table, buying groceries, chatting with Evi's mom, without ever letting on to us? I'm crying for you, Mom, and a bit for Laura too, because obviously she's next. But I'm also crying for Dad, because I love him, and I can't reconcile this love with everything I now know. I can be angry at him, but I can't hate him. To be honest, I'd love to crawl up against him and his big strong back just like in the old days, but it seems that spot was never actually empty for long. How many women have lain there beside him? What were they thinking? That they'd been chosen, or special? Will I be doing the same thing later on in my life? Will I ever consider a man so important that having him is the only thing that matters?*

I'm startled when my bedroom door gently opens all of a sudden.

"Oh my God, Luuk, what're you doing?" He's crying. I leap out of bed and throw my arms around him.

"I wet my bed," he says and sniffles. My heart breaks. He hasn't done this in months. "I don't want to wake up Dad."

"No, sweetie, come here, we'll change your bed together."

"Why aren't you sleeping?"

"I can't."

We creep into the hallway together, Luuk without his pajama bottoms. "You take a shower and I'll clean up the bed."

"They'll wake up."

"It's not that big a deal, Luuk."

"Yes it is. I don't want them to know."

"I'm sure they won't mind. It's not such a strange thing to happen, with everything that's going on now, is it?"

I take him to the bathroom and turn on the shower. The light hurts my eyes. Luuk has a tall body for his age, but inside he's just a kid who's often overlooked. I kiss his cheek and say what grown-ups say: "It's going to be alright, Luuk."

"I want Mom. I want her so bad everything hurts, and I can't stop thinking about where she might be, especially when it's dark and raining. What if she's dead and lying somewhere all alone?" He starts crying again.

"She's not dead. Really."

"Wouldn't she have been back a long time ago if she wasn't?"

Someone knocks on the bathroom door.

"Everything's under control here!" I cry. My throat is starting to swell. I feel like breaking down too.

"Alright," Laura calls back.

"I don't want to go to school tomorrow," Luuk says to me.

"I don't either."

I take off my nightgown and step into the shower to help him, and Luuk and I grab on to each other like monkeys. We cry, but we laugh too. "I'm so glad I have you," Luuk says. "You're kind of, like, the only thing that's normal. Or the only thing that's left from the old days. Do you hate Laura too?"

"Yeah. But it's not her fault." And I wish I didn't know whose fault it is.

When we walk into Luuk's room all clean and dry, Laura's just finished changing his sheets. "The wash is going already," she says, nervously eyeing us, hoping for kindness. Luuk slides into bed without looking at her. I know it's because he's ashamed, but Laura will take it as a lack of gratitude.

"That's cool of you," I say.

"I used to do it too, you know," Laura says. "It's nothing to be ashamed of."

The Grown-Up

We hear Chonk barking downstairs.

"Oh God." Laura gives me a startled look. "Come on, guys, it's really late already. Good night, Luuk. Alright, Lies, back to bed."

Chonk is really hollering now.

"Shouldn't we go see what's up?" I ask.

"It's your father," Laura says. "He was out."

Imagine waking up and right away thinking: something's up. *Mom's gone.* How are you supposed to sleep if your mom's missing? I feel like there's a millstone of guilt around my neck. *Mom.* I need to find God in her story. I reach for my MacBook.

Downstairs, the doorbell rings. Is it her? Is it someone who knows where she is? My heart beats like I just ran a half marathon. I run downstairs in my bathrobe and slippers, and I'm jumped on by a completely hysterical Chonk. I can hear there are people in the living room. Laura's standing at the bottom of the stairs, white as a ghost. Without makeup, her face resembles an egg. She apparently has to paint on any expression by hand.

"Go get your father," she says. She sounds out of breath. I feel as if I'm standing beside myself again, just like when Mom and Dad told us they were getting a divorce.

I watch myself get Dad out of bed, the smell of alcohol permeating the bedroom, Dad groaning and initially unwilling to get up. I hear myself say, "I think it's something bad." Do I know already? No. But I could tell something from Laura's voice. I see myself going to Luuk's room. "Come on, you need to come right now. There's people."

"Is it Mom?" No. Or maybe it is. One of the voices sounded like a woman. But if it was Mom, wouldn't she have been the one standing at the bottom of the stairs? Maybe it's people who'll bring us to her. "Right, from the hospital," Luuk says. It's possible. She's in the hospital. Only, Dad called all the hospitals in the area already. A hospital far away? Who knows? "Hurry up. They're waiting."

They're in the room, Jochem the police officer and his female colleague. They're holding their caps. Their expressions give nothing away, but I can see Jochem's jaw quiver.

"We have some bad news," he says.

Dad sits down. He looks ridiculous in his brown terry bathrobe, his eyes bloodshot and puffy. Luuk's standing behind me, his arms wrapped around my waist. I look around the group and try with all my might to suppress my rising panic.

"She's been found."

14.

I feel as if I've been uncorked. I hear a high whistle in my ear. None of us move. Dad has his face in his hands. Laura's back is against the countertop. Luuk and I stand in the middle of the room, opposite the officers now staring at the floor. I want to kick someone. Dad, preferably. In the face, so his teeth go flying. The way he's sitting there with his hangover.

"How? Where?" Laura's the first to talk. Luuk goes over to Dad and leans against him. No one's crying. All I can do is take deep breaths.

"A cleaner found her in a holiday cottage in Sparrenburg."

"We have to call Grandma," I say.

"You can call anyone you want," says the female officer whose name I've already forgotten again.

"And Kim."

"Peter, is there anyone else you want to call?" Laura asks. "Friends? Your business partner perhaps?"

Dad gets up and runs to the hallway. We hear him throw up in the toilet.

"Oh my God, poor children," Laura says. "How awful. I'm completely . . . I can't believe it. What should I do? What should I do?" She waves her hands in the air and then moves toward me. I dodge her attempt to give me a hug. The fact that she's here at this moment is unbearable. This all started with her.

"How? How can she be . . ." I can't say the word.

"We'll wait until everyone involved is here," Jochem says.

"Perhaps you and your brother would like to go be with a friend?" the female officer asks.

"We don't want to go anywhere," I say. That's what grown-ups always do in emergency situations: try and leave you with someone else.

"Sweeties," Laura says, "perhaps it's better if the police talk with Dad and Grandma first. I don't know if what they have to say is suitable for children."

"Shut up, Laura," I say. "You're a child too."

Grandma and Kim come bursting in. Chonk is barking and running through the room. Luuk and I crawl onto Grandma's lap. She's trembling. Dad returns from the bathroom. He wants to give Grandma a kiss, but she shrinks back. "Maybe you should make yourself a bit presentable," she says.

Dad's chin starts to tremble. "I'm so sorry for you, Tineke. And for you, my sweet, beautiful kids."

"And for yourself," I say.

"That too," he says.

"What happened?" Grandma asks. Laura hands her a cup of coffee.

"Are you sure the children should be here for this?" Jochem asks. I still think he's handsome, but he thinks I'm a child.

"We're old enough," I say.

"They'll find out one way or another," Grandma says.

"It appears that Jet took her own life in a cottage in Sparrenburg."

Only now do we start to cry, all of us at the same time, triggered by Grandma's primal scream. Only now has it become real. Mom's dead. Luuk and I hold each other tight and shiver. "This can't be. Not again," Grandma says. Dad runs to Laura as the female officer covers her mouth. Chonk jumps on us, yowling. We drag each other down, deeper and deeper. The female officer pours glasses of water and pats our backs in sympathy, but after a while the crying stops just as suddenly as it began. We take deep breaths and grab the tissues Kim hands us. We hear each other's quivering sighs, and for a moment I feel a deep connection with everyone in the room, even Laura.

"Can I see her?" Grandma asks.

"Of course. You can come with us to identify her."

"So you're not even certain it's her?"

"We're almost certain, but only next of kin can confirm it."

"How did she do it?" Dad asks.

"By drowning, we suspect. She was found in the bath. There aren't any bottles or other signs that she overdosed on medication."

I look at Luuk, who's even paler than normal, almost green. He looks at me with hollow eyes and whispers: "Didn't I tell you? She really was dead. And she was lying all by herself. In a cold bath."

Grandma goes to the station with Dad, which is rather complicated because they're arguing. Luuk and I stay home with Laura and Kim, which is complicated in a different way. Luckily, Laura's not saying anything. Kim is sitting opposite me on the tip of the armchair. Luuk asks if it's alright if he plays a video game, and everyone agrees it's fine. He then asks if it's silly to play games when your mother just died. I think it is, actually, but Laura and Kim don't. There aren't any rules for how to behave after hearing the worst possible news of your life. I'm afraid to do anything other than sit there, staring at the glass side table, thinking about Mom's final hours.

"I don't believe any of it," I say to Kim.

"I'm afraid it's true, dear."

"No, I mean about the suicide."

She looks at me, her jaws tensed. "I can't believe it myself yet either. But your mom was definitely feeling a bit low lately. I feel so incredibly stupid for not noticing how low. What a hard time she was having. I misjudged completely. It seemed like she was picking herself back up."

On that last word, she casts a glance at Laura.

"This was her way of wounding Peter forever," Laura says with her back toward us, resting against the hard stone counter. "The ultimate revenge."

"She was murdered," I say. "Mom was murdered. I'm positive."

Laura turns around.

Kim grabs my hands. "Honey, I understand why you'd want to think that. But by who? And why?"

They're not taking me seriously.

"She would never do this, leave us alone at night. She said she never forgave her father for killing himself. She feels people with children are obliged to go on living, no matter how depressed they are. It's no longer about you when you have children, she said. What matters is that you're there, as a zombie if need be."

Kim looks at me, teary-eyed. Her face is red and gray at the same time. "I think your mom couldn't think straight anymore. Depression is a type of illness."

"Right," Laura says. "I've had it myself, a breakdown. It's awful. I felt I'd rather die than go on living the way I was."

"We're not talking about you now," Kim says. "I don't think there's anything anyone could have done. Her father had it too. She fought like a tiger."

I stare at my black slippers. Mom gave them to me for Christmas, even though she hardly had any money. *It's important to keep your feet warm*, she said, *especially if you regularly have bladder infections.* I always take them with me, back and forth, in my backpack.

The doorbell rings. Laura checks to see who's there. "It's just my parents!" she calls and runs into the hallway.

"Poor child," Kim says.

"Why isn't *she* dead?" I scream and run to my room, the room I hate.

15.

My sadness is too big for me to cry. And it's still possible that it isn't true. That it's another woman they found. That's why I need to look for God in Mom's words. There has to be a clue somewhere here, something to prove what they're saying downstairs is wrong. I lie down in bed on my stomach and read. I can picture her as I do. She's in the corner by the window in the wicker chair, her hands clutching a cup of coffee. *We know all about the divorce already, Mom, so when did you meet God?*

Another night by myself. For a while, I looked forward to my evenings, to changing from my work clothes into my sweats, T-shirt, fleece sweater, no makeup, face cream on, my hair in a bun. I ate readymade meals straight out of the container in front of the television, with red wine. I'd binge whole seasons of The Affair *and* The Good Wife, *tucked under my blanket, until I fell asleep. Then I'd wake up in the middle of the night in a kind of panic and immediately take a Xanax to turn off my anxiety.*

At that point I'd started to see how sad my new life really was. I was active and engaged one week when I was with the kids, cooking healthy, whistling along to music, then living as if on hold the week after, glum and lethargic. I'd promised my kids I wouldn't start a relationship as long as they lived at home, but that wasn't realistic, of course. Not that I wanted a relationship. I wanted my family back, preferably in its old, familiar form. I couldn't bear to think of a new man, of being in love and the terrible insecurities that brings.

What I did want was to be touched. Sex. A body next to me, inside me, on top of me. To be seen by eyes other than my children's. Someone to pick myself up off the sofa for. So one evening after three glasses of wine, I finally went to that virtual meeting place for lonely souls and set up a Tinder account.

It wasn't a pretty sight. A never-ending stream of selfies, bald heads, often with sunglasses and hats, men on boats, next to bikes or motorcycles, or in front of a barbecue. Men with expensive watches, dogs, ripped physiques, young children, tattoos, half beards. At the beach, nursing beers. Bodies without faces. I forced myself to like a couple. I figured it couldn't hurt, tried to see it as practice material, as entertainment. Told myself I had nothing to lose.

I swiped right on a guy named Bart, forty-nine, because of his blue eyes and blond hair. I did the same for Tom, forty-five, a cool guy with a hat, staring at a setting sun, and a mysterious man who called himself God, because his name made me laugh. He was forty-one, had a dark beard and wore a white suit and black sunglasses. Plays Tinder on level 9, his bio read.

It turned out I matched with all three. Even though I knew this didn't mean anything, I felt uplifted for a minute anyway. I'd been seen.

The following morning I woke in a silent house, in a bed too big, my head groggy. I just couldn't get used to the emptiness, even with Chonk at my side.

I checked my phone. I had three messages. Hey pretty lady, *Tom wrote, and something about me looking vulnerable.* Hi, what are you up to? *Bart wrote.* And the third: Good morning, beautiful. What a pleasant surprise that we're a match. Let me know if you want to meet up some time. I don't really like chatting endlessly. In my experience, that only makes the gap between expectations and reality even wider. And at the end of the day, I think we both want the same thing. Realness. To be seen and touched. Oh. God.

A man who called himself God. I thought that was funny.

"What exactly do you mean with 'plays Tinder on level 9'?" I replied.

When I went out to walk Chonk, I seemed to have brightened a bit.

Dad and Grandma are back. Grandma seems a hundred years old. She's trembling. Dad silently stares into the distance. He looks ashen. Laura pours wine while Kim makes sandwiches no one eats. Chonk is lying by the front door, panting. Mom won't ever come to get him anymore. This "anymore" is something I just can't get my head around. In my mind, she's at home, waiting for us to come back, the same feeling I always have when I'm here: *We need to go to her. Our life is where she is.* No one dares say anything.

"It's your child, you know," Grandma says suddenly. "It's still . . . no matter how old she is. It's my child. I can still picture her as a baby, as a toddler. I see her hopping on her bicycle, waving. Always cheerful. And so bright." She shakes her head, then lets it hang. "When Felix died . . ." She takes a deep breath and pauses a long time.

Kim and I exchange a glance, and then she gestures at me with her head. I take Grandma's hand, and she pulls me close.

"I may have neglected her a little during that time. She was thirteen, a difficult time. The hardest age for a young girl, and then her father dies? It was hard to handle her. She was so angry. To think that later she would . . . I don't understand. She knows what it's like."

"There was a letter," Dad says.

The ensuing silence makes me want to scream, tear the linen curtains off the rod. A letter, goddammit. She didn't write it. Why doesn't anyone say this?

"I wasn't allowed to take it with me. It has to stay in the file for some time still, but I took a picture."

He gets his phone.

I can't stand this any longer, I need to get away. I'm spent, hollow inside. Please leave me alone forever. I understand it's difficult, it hurts, and I'm really sorry. It hurts me too. But if you really love me, you'll respect my decision. It's the only way out I can see anymore.

"And then three *x*'s, for kisses. Handwritten. It was on the nightstand by the bed. In that cottage where she . . ."

"That isn't necessarily a suicide note, though, is it?" Kim says. "It could be anything."

"That's right!" I say, relieved that at least one adult here has her doubts.

"It's her handwriting," Dad says.

"Sure. I just find it very strange."

"She didn't have her wits about her, Kim. She smashed the patio door."

"How can we be so sure she's the one who did that?" Kim asks.

"She was running through the field behind the house without any clothes on. People saw her."

"And no one went up to her or tried to help?"

Dad shakes his head.

"She's speaking to someone in that letter," Kim says.

"Me, I think," he says.

"Her life had stopped revolving around you a long time ago," she says.

"It's revenge, Kim. The best way to ruin my life. *How can I make sure he'll never, ever be happy again?* Well, like this!"

Grandma holds me closer still. "Could you please control yourself a little?" she says to him.

I wonder if I should bring up God. This letter was meant for him, I'm sure of it.

"This letter isn't for you, Dad. Mom knew a man, and I think it was for him."

Dad breathes in deep through his nose, then puts his face in his hands.

The Grown-Up

"I know she went on a few dates," Grandma says. "She liked one of them, but he was a bit of a loon. She said so herself. She never mentioned him again after that. The letter Felix wrote was cryptic too. They're not all there at that point, are they? Felix was having hallucinations . . . The doctor would only give him three sleeping pills at a time. He was able to collect enough anyway." She's mostly talking to herself.

"You can just order drugs online these days," Dad says.

"He'd been stockpiling them. For years. Even his mother's own tramadol," Grandma continues.

"Combined drug intoxication," Dad says.

"What's that?" Laura asks.

"When you take a bunch of different pills. What Jet must have done. Like her father."

I picture the pill bottles in our medicine cabinet. It was true that Mom had been sleeping poorly.

"In her line of work, she could have gotten as much as she needed." Dad starts to cry. We're all silent. Grandma leans toward him and puts her hand on his knee.

"I couldn't accept it," she says. "We had such a nice life, such love. A beautiful daughter."

I wish she would stop going on about a grandpa I never knew. What does he matter? That was a thousand years ago. My mother's dead. Right now.

"Mom wasn't depressed or having hallucinations or whatever," I say. "She slept poorly at times, felt stressed occasionally, but she's a psychologist, so she'd know perfectly well how to deal with that." My words don't seem to affect anyone.

"All she wanted was to understand her father's suicide. That's why she went on to study psychology."

Grandma needs to shut up right now.

Laura gets up to hide behind the kitchen island with her mother. Luuk comes over to sit with me and puts his arms around my neck.

His skinny legs hang between mine, like a toddler's. How are we to go on now? Where do we start? It feels like we've been sitting in this low-oxygen room like this for centuries, stuck with each other, watched by intruders—especially Laura, and it's her fault we're sitting here at all.

16.

On Kim's advice, I've agreed to meet up with all three matches. I already know who piques my curiosity the most, but she says I should spread out the opportunities and risk. *Never put all your eggs in one basket,* she says. She should know, since she plays Tinder on level ten, as God would put it. Three dates, three coffee meetups at my favorite old haunt in Amsterdam. *An hour per date at most,* Kim says, *and save the food and drink for a second meeting. Tell them the deal right away at the end, don't keep them hanging. You'll know if it's something within seconds. You have plenty of friends already.* This last part isn't true; the only one I still have is Kim, but she's right that I'm not on Tinder to collect friends. Nor to find a relationship. I want a dependable sex partner, someone I find attractive but who I won't fall in love with. Someone I can go see on lonely nights but who'll leave me alone during my happy weeks with the kids. I know perfectly well that this goal comes with risks: I've never *not* fallen in love with a man I have good sex with.

But this time I'll try to see it just as a fun way to pass the time, a way to connect with men every now and then without strings, without having to answer to someone, and especially without handing them my heart on a silver platter.

Tom's already sitting at a table by the window when I enter. He's balding under his hat and at least ten years older than he looked in his profile picture. He's wearing a grayish T-shirt and a taupe hooded vest. Brown leather Campers with beige shoelaces. He gets up when he sees me, and we greet each other with three kisses, bumping our foreheads a bit too hard on the last one. We both take a seat, carefully avoiding each other's eyes, and I wonder if he finds me disappointing too. I've shaved myself literally from top to bottom, blow-dried my hair with the round brush. I'm wearing my gold earrings, red high heels, and the dress I bought for a wedding last year because I knew Peter would be there with Laura, and I wanted to look better than her at all costs. My nails are polished, and I worked on my makeup for a full hour. Clearly excessive for a Friday morning at half past ten. Overeager. Now he'll think I'm superficial, concerned only with appearances, which certainly can't be said of him. We chat about the location, which Tom finds original, and I tell him I used to come here all the time, before my kids, before the divorce, before my life came to a grinding halt. "It's even more fun during the evening," I hear myself say. Tom answers that he hopes he'll be able to experience that with me for himself sometime. *Too fast, too soon,* Kim says inside my head.

Tom has two children who live with him every other week. He's on good terms with his ex; they even live next door to each other. There's nothing, absolutely nothing attractive about him. I can't imagine running my tongue along his crooked, uneven lower teeth, or feeling his flabby buttocks in my hands, that balding head between my breasts. He tells me he's a manager for a big textile manufacturer and has just gotten a new car. He'll be watching soccer with friends this evening, and he's quite nervous about that. Even more nervous than about this date, ha ha, because PSV has to win. It seems he's for PSV while his whole family is for Ajax. He doesn't ask many questions but shows me photos of his children. There's something sleazy about staring at someone else's kids already and being expected to say they look cute. It's like I'm being unfaithful to Lies and Luuk, which is why I don't want to show him their pictures. What I really want to do is leave.

Hey, Tom, it was nice meeting you, but I don't think we click. Shall we pay the tab?

The Grown-Up

I don't have the nerve to say it. I'm incapable of rejecting even a man I'll never see again, who I don't even like, a total stranger I have no connection with. So we drink three cappuccinos and eat apple pie, and he tells me all about his autistic son and his favorite place to go camping in Ardèche, before he asks me for my number so he can text me for a next date. He really has to go now and never thought time would fly like this. *That's a good sign, right?*

I give him my number and decide to reject him later via WhatsApp.

Back in my car, I cry. Other people may find this process fun and exciting, but I feel like a failure. Violated, even. *Good God, Jet, it's just a date,* Kim says. I don't want to be getting coffee with complete strangers, wondering the whole time whether I'd be able to bring myself to fuck them when I know they're asking themselves the same thing. I want familiarity. My desire for what I used to have is almost tangible. Drinking coffee together without talking. All of us in one house, on one street just around the corner from here. The thought of being condemned to this now, to men like Tom . . . How could I have liked someone like that? What's wrong with me?

I buy cigarettes on my way home. A dramatic gesture, I'm aware. I also take a Xanax and order food from the only place that delivers in this neighborhood: the Chinese restaurant. Mu shu pork. Pathetic, but by this point I've numbed myself so much I don't even care.

I close my MacBook, not wanting to read any more. My face in my hands, I try to gather myself so I can face the soap opera unfolding downstairs. When I get down there, everyone's hanging around, drinking, eating, talking. Everyone acts like they know a thousand things about my mother, but I'm sure I know her better than all of them put together. Better than her own mother, even. Better than my father. Despite this, she'd partly become a stranger to me too over this past year. I nearly throw up at the thought of her being so sad and lonely. *You two are the only light in my life.* She said this occasionally, but I refused to hear it because what do you say to that? To her misery, to Dad's annoyance with it? I figured it would stop someday, like it had with all my other classmates' parents. All of a sudden, they'd no longer be angry and would become friends. But that day will never come now. In our hearts, she'll always be lonely, angry, sad, and abandoned.

At one time, though, there were summers in the city with the balcony doors open, the barbecue on the balcony. Mom had made a spot in the shade with batik cloths, and there was a hammock. They were still comfortable touching each other then. We played on the sidewalk where the neighbors were sitting too, drinking wine. Dad laughed, put his arm around her shoulders, and kissed her forehead. I never thought about them at the time. They were just there, my parents, living with and loving each other. Dad wore an apron over his bare chest and pricked the sausages with a long fork. Mom put salad and sauce trays on the little table. "A bit meager," she would say, and Dad would answer: "There's enough to feed a whole orphanage."

He says the same line now to Laura, who's started cooking like crazy. There are some new people in the room. I don't know them. They introduce themselves, but I forget their names and ignore their pity, their eyes full of unhelpful tears, the consoling shoulder squeezes.

"Can't we just be alone with each other for a while?" I whisper, leaning against Dad.

"These people want to show their support," he says.

"But I don't know them."

"They're colleagues, neighbors, friends of Laura's, friends of mine, Laura's brother and his girlfriend."

It's quite a party.

"But you know what?" he says. "Why don't we go for a walk with Chonk, just the three of us, alright?"

Luuk protests but then throws his controller aside. We go out wearing our coats as it's quite cold. We walk along the always-windy street to the park, Luuk with his hands in his pockets, me locking arms with Dad. I chain myself to him, wanting him all for myself, the only parent I have left.

"Dad, are you actually sad?" Luuk asks.

The Grown-Up

"Of course, Luuk. I'm very, very sad."

"Oh. Good. I thought maybe, because you're divorced and always saying how stupid Mom is, you'd be happy."

Dad keeps silent for some time. There are grooves in his cheeks, and his once-shiny black hair is turning gray. Over the last year, he's posted Instagram stories from the gym, wearing a neon yellow shirt and a band in his hair. When he's off to this or that techno concert, he'll show off his wristband for Awakenings, or backstage at Mysteryland. Evi and I find it super cringey. He also has a rather stupid haircut these days, like soccer players have, shaved on the side with a kind of quiff on top, which makes him look like an old parakeet. Mom would often joke about it, and I'd laugh with her, even though I'd feel a kind of pang too.

Dad's crying now, his chin trembling.

"Oh my God, Luuk, of course Dad's sad." I take Dad's hand.

"I don't think Mom's stupid. I think it's stupid we got so . . . that it went like this. That we argued. We just couldn't work it out. I loved Mom very much. Very, very much."

Now Luuk and I are crying too. Because Mom can't hear him say this anymore.

In the park, we throw the ball to Chonk, who can't get enough of it. After a while, Dad and I sit down on a bench while Luuk keeps running and throwing.

"I feel so guilty, Lies."

He sounds like he's talking to an adult. I sit up straight.

"Could I have prevented it? Did she do it to get back at me? How could she do this? Leave you two behind like this? She knows what that's like . . ."

"Do you remember what it was like when we were all together still? In Amsterdam? You loved each other then." I prefer to talk about the past, the nice things.

Dad nods and chuckles. He remembers too, I think. "Such a tiny house."

"But so cozy."

"I bet it's worth a whole lot more now."

"I miss it. The school and the bakery." And us. "Don't you ever miss it?"

"Of course. The family, the familiarity. You two around me every day." He's resting his elbows on his knees and holding his head in his hands. "Oh God," he cries, his voice breaking. Tears land between his feet, and snot runs from his nose. Is he crying over the past, for Mom, or for himself? It's strange how they would say the worst things about each other but never wanted to say where it actually went wrong. All of a sudden, Luuk and I would be "too young" to hear about it. All I know is Dad suddenly needed some space, and then there was Laura, who turned out to have been there for some years already. From that moment on, Mom and Dad hated each other.

"I don't think she did it herself," I say, hoping to soothe his pain a little.

He puts his arms around me and holds me close. I can smell his sweat, together with the fragrant pomade he puts in his hair.

"I understand why you'd think that, but we need to accept it, Lies, as hard as it is. She chose this. She wanted peace. I think she just couldn't go on any longer."

"She was cheerful and sweet this past week. Not depressed or angry. I could see she was picking her life back up. She was cooking nice things and buying flowers. Luuk and I both got new clothes . . ."

"That's a sign, apparently. Giving gifts, creating beautiful moments. It's like a goodbye ritual."

I free myself from his grip while Luuk tries to fish the ball out of the water with a stick. Chonk is barking.

"It was her job to help depressed people," I say. "She'd know what to do if all of a sudden she wanted to kill herself, wouldn't she?"

"She was obsessed with suicide because of your grandpa. It's a bit like a fear of heights: you're scared of heights, but you're also inclined to jump."

"You think I need to accept that she killed herself, but I think it's strange how quick you are to believe it. Honestly, Dad, I know her better than you do. Mom would never do this to us. Exactly because of Grandpa."

Luuk returns, trailing behind him a dripping-wet Chonk, who eagerly jumps onto Dad's lap. I can hear Mom burst out laughing: "Good for you."

I need to go to bed, but how am I supposed to sleep when my mother is lying in a cold drawer somewhere? My head is nearly exploding with images: her dead body on a steel table. A pathologist cutting out her organs. Mom in the bath, her hands and feet wrinkled by the water. Blue skin in red water, perhaps. Did she cut herself? Or did she really drown? An overdose? No one's telling me what happened. I try to imagine how I'd go about it. Most likely with pills, like Dad said. Fall asleep and never wake up. Maybe Mom did wake up again, and she didn't really mean to do it. She didn't want to die, but she didn't have a phone with her and there was no one else around. A burst of panic, struggling not to slip away. She threw a chair through the patio door, ran into the field. People saw her but didn't do anything. Only, none of it makes sense. Did she get back into the bath, resigned at the end? Mom loved us. We made her happy. She wasn't the type to think *My children are better off without me.* She knew she was a good mother. She was convinced we couldn't live without her. And we can't.

I stare at the dark silhouettes in my room when my phone lights up. A WhatsApp message. It's Mees. Only now, after I'd nearly forgotten him.

> Hi! That's fucked up about your mother. I bet you're real sad. Is it cool if I come by tomorrow?

No doubt Evi told him to do this. Because I'm sad. In any case, it's not because he loves me like I love him. We kissed in the park near my old house, my family's real house, after he and I had drunk vanilla vodka with the rest of our group. I'm always too chicken to do anything, but not when I've had something to drink. All of a sudden, I had the nerve to walk home with him. His parents are divorced too, but they're still the best of friends. His mother's boyfriend watches soccer with his father. Mees said that's awkward sometimes.

"When they argue, it's obvious why they separated," he said.

"I'd kill to have my parents be friends," I said.

"Who would you kill?" he asked.

"Laura," I said. This made him laugh, and I pretended to laugh too, and then he put his arm around my neck and pulled me toward him. Casually, as if he did such things every day. I tried to act as relaxed as possible, and then I felt his soft lips on mine. I could smell vanilla, alcohol, and his Axe deodorant. His tongue slipped into my mouth like a small fish. I opened my mouth as wide as possible and held my head at an angle, like I'd practiced with Evi months ago. My tongue was making circles around his. His breath on my cheeks. He was grinding his pelvis against my thigh, and I felt a strange sense of shame. He could feel my fat now, my breasts, which are too small. I worried that I smelled of urine because I get bladder infections so often.

"I have to get home," I kept saying. "So do I," he said. But we kept going. His hand underneath my sweater, fumbling with my bra strap. "I'm going home now," I said all of a sudden, and I pushed him away. My whole body felt swollen and sticky. I also had hair down there, and I worried he'd be able to feel it.

Back home in the shower, I ran my hand through my crotch and smelled it. It smelled odd, not of fish like everyone says, but of soil and iron and steak. Had he smelled this too? The embarrassment rose up within me until I was bright red and full of blotches. Mom came into the bathroom, and I quickly put away the razor.

"Why are you home so late?" she asked.

"I was at the park with Evi, and we lost track of time."

She stood next to the shower. "I can't sleep when I don't know where you are. Next time just send me a message saying where you are and who you're with."

"I was with Mees too," I blurted out. I didn't feel ashamed in front of her. We were like one.

"Oh! How was it? Did you talk? Was he nice?"

"We kissed."

"Ah . . . Oh my! How wonderful! And now what?"

"What do you mean, 'And now what?'"

"Are you going steady?"

"Of course not."

"Would you want to?"

My cheeks were turning red again. "I don't think he does."

"You can't know, sweetie, unless you ask."

"No way. And please don't say anything to Jolande." Mom knew his mother, and so did Kim.

She stared at me and smiled. "Well, let's get some rest, then. I bet you'll have sweet dreams."

I turned off the shower, and she handed me a towel. "You're beautiful, sweet Lies. Don't let anyone ever tell you otherwise."

But apparently, we weren't like one person after all. She kept secrets from me.

I agree to meet Bart in the same café at the same time, on a different day. He turns out to have been a client of mine some years ago. We both have a good laugh about not recognizing each other's profile photos. But now that he's here at a table in the sun, I can recall his painful divorce again, his sleeplessness and depression. He was done with life, he said at the time. But here he is, a pound or two heavier than in his profile picture, wearing a sweater that's a bit too tight. He has red hair and a red beard, which looked a bit darker in his picture, and a pair of overly thick-framed black glasses on his nose.

"At least we don't have to go through the awkwardness of introducing ourselves," he says. "But my God, it's not the best endorsement, obviously. You've seen me at my worst."

"Not worst," I say. *"Vulnerable."* Right away, I slip back into my role as his therapist.

"Can we still have coffee, or do you want to go home right now?"

I laugh away my disappointment. *"We'll have coffee, of course. It's great to see you're doing well, Bart."*

Bart had suddenly stopped coming to therapy, no longer answered emails or phone calls, and hadn't responded to invoices.

"Oh man, I'm so embarrassed."

"I was worried about you."

"Understandable. It became too much for me, all that digging in my soul. I wasn't ready for it yet. I lost myself in drinking and drugs for a while, but that's all behind me now. I'm clean and talking to my ex again. The kids are doing great. But you! To think you're on Tinder!"

"I'll be going off it again, though. I think it's awful."

"Ha ha, that's what everyone says. I actually think it's kind of fun. You shouldn't take it so seriously. Just see it as pure entertainment. And sometimes you get lucky."

"Sex, you mean?"

"Sex, or a really good conversation."

"It's just your luck now to run into your old shrink. And to have to pay that last invoice."

Bart doubles over with laughter. *"Oh man, sweet karma."*

Our coffee is served, and the waitress gives me a sardonic look. She was working when I was here with Tom too.

"Obviously, I'll pay it. I'm so embarrassed."

We both take a sip of our cappuccinos, and I momentarily slip back into that strange dark feeling I had after my last date, which makes it impossible for me to look at Bart. I want to run, away from all this.

"But sorry to hear it happened to you too. That's screwed up. I mean it, I always thought: That Jet, she has it all figured out. She knows how to do it, keep a relationship going well."

"Apparently not. I'm only human, and so is my ex-husband."

"Where did it go wrong? And please, spare me the therapeutic version."

I chuckle. The darkness has subsided again. "It's a cliché story. He was made a partner and began working more and more, and I felt cast aside. We stopped being intimate, and then all of a sudden he wanted to live alone for a while and think. There was someone else, of course, but he didn't say so until we went on our last family vacation. I thought a trip might bring us closer together again. He thought it was the perfect time to admit he was having an affair with Laura."

"Oh," Bart says. He picks at a beer mat. His wife had been seeing someone else, which she was quite open about, but he couldn't deal with it and fell into a deep, dark depression, which his wife couldn't deal with. They came to those first sessions together, but later he always came alone because his wife felt he needed therapy more than she did.

"Did it make things easier that it's your job, helping people with their relationships?"

"Not at all. I stepped in every land mine. We're not talking to each other at all right now. I think I hate him. Because it's such a cliché, running off with a chick who's fifteen years younger. We're fighting in court over money, and he's a lawyer so you can imagine what that's like. Now he wants full custody because he thinks I'm neglecting the kids. He's turned into a complete stranger."

"And your kids? How are they handling it?"

"Very well, actually. Kids are so flexible. They want both of us to be happy, that's all. I don't think they really like living with him every other week, but they're also afraid to choose."

"Do you really hate it when they're gone?"

"It's awful. Every time he comes to get them, it's like my heart is being torn out."

"Yes," he says. The beer mat is on the table in a hundred pieces. "You get used to it. But it stays . . . I can picture it, my kids at that table with that man playing the cool stepdad. This isn't the dream it all began with. I saw them crawl out of her . . . Separation isn't easy for a father either."

"I know. But mothers give birth to their kids. I know it's not very enlightened of me, but I feel children belong with their mother. It's how nature designed it. Those bonds are made of blood."

Bart's face tightens. "That's ridiculous. It feels like an amputation to me too, every time I see them leave. Good thing Keesje will be moving out to the city, and so will Levi next year. Then that'll be the end of all this back and forth."

"Children belong with their mother."

That's right, Mom, so where are you now?

I shut my MacBook and hold it against my chest, as if Mom's inside, alive and well. My mother, talking to me from beyond death. I can almost smell her, that scent of sleep I found a bit offensive not too long ago, feel those soft arms, her hair prickly against my cheek. My eyes are tired, my head pounding. Where is she? Who did this? How will I ever be normal again? Am I allowed to meet with Mees? Am I allowed to like things still, or go to school, or go out, or do anything else besides being stuck in this fucking apartment with Grandma and Laura's family? And Luuk, poor Luuk. He's still so young. What's going to happen with him? I wish I was old enough to go back to our real house, with Luuk, so I could take care of him instead of that horrible Laura. I don't know if I'm awake or dreaming, but all of a sudden I picture Laura pushing Mom underwater in a bath. Her perfect fingernails on Mom's face.

I startle myself, like I just fell from a great height, and all of a sudden I'm wide awake with my heart pounding like mad. I get my pillow, walk through the dark hallway to Luuk's room and get in bed beside him. He pushes his warm little body back against mine. I kiss his hair, like Mom would.

"Don't wet your bed now, okay?" I say.

17.

"Lies! There's a boy here for you!" Dad cries from downstairs.

New people keep showing up to participate in the uncomfortable silence. Laura's mother keeps making sandwiches. I'm sick of her "famous" tomato soup with meatballs. The whole house reeks of it. Luuk is permitted to play video games in his room now, something Mom would never have allowed. Chonk is lying on my bed with me.

I jump up and throw on my yellow Adidas sweatpants and blue hoodie. I tie my hair in a knot and gloss my lips. Dad calls out again. I look in the mirror: I'm as white as chalk and have dark rings under my eyes. I go downstairs, and there he is, holding a bunch of flowers. Mees looks even more handsome than usual in his jean jacket. He briefly smiles, then looks embarrassed, after which he gives me a solemn look.

"Hey," he says.

My eyes fill with tears, from sadness but also nervousness. He gives me a hug and kisses my neck.

"It's fucked up," he says. "I'm so, so sorry."

I nod and take the flowers, trying to avoid his glance as best I can. I have no idea how to do this. I'm sad. I'm in love.

"Do you want some soup?" I ask. I put my hand on my neck, on the spot he just kissed, which now feels like it's burning.

"Yeah, sure."

Everyone falls silent when we walk in. I'm in no mood for shaking hands with this new load of strangers. "This is Mees," I say. We make our way to the kitchen island, where Laura and her mother are frantically puttering about. "Can we have a bowl of soup?"

"Of course!" Laura says in that voice she uses especially for kids. She extends her hand to Mees, and he offers her his condolences. She then winks at me. Stupid woman.

We eat our soup on the edge of my bed.

"Nice apartment," Mees says.

"Yeah," I say. "But I like Mom's house more. It's cozier."

"Mothers are better at that, making things cozy. Mine's helping my father decorate his place now. He's moving." I can see him turn red. "Sorry," he says.

"What for?"

"Talking about my mother."

"It's alright."

We're quiet for a minute. Mees puts the last meatball in his mouth. "Good soup."

I put my full bowl on the nightstand. "It's disgusting soup. Laura's fucking parents made it, and they're never leaving." I don't have the energy to eat or act tough. More than anything, I'd like to rest my head on his lap and fall asleep as he caresses my hair. "I don't believe my mom killed herself." I let myself fall back onto the bed.

He stays seated and puts his empty bowl on the floor. "I wouldn't be able to believe it either," he says.

"I think I can prove it too."

"Did you say that to the police?"

"Yes, and to my dad, but they think it's ridiculous. They're thinking: scorned woman, obviously depressed, her father committed suicide too, access to all kinds of scary pills, it's clear as day."

"My mother said there was a note."

"A vague note. I'm sure that if she'd really wanted to take her own life, she'd have written us personal letters. Plus Mom became a therapist to help people who plan to kill themselves. It was because of her father that she knows what this does to children."

The Grown-Up

"Hey, I believe you. But my mother said there's a kind of short-circuiting of your brain, that you can feel so desperate you think everyone's better off without you. A bit like being in some dense fog. She said it's an illness."

"Your mother knows a lot, doesn't she?"

He doesn't get that I'm being sarcastic. A turnoff that I decide to overlook for now.

"Yeah, my mom has talked to Kim a lot. She's heartbroken. Nobody saw it coming."

"My mom was murdered, Mees. Her MacBook and her phone were wiped clean. She was dating this guy, God."

He moves back and sits beside me, then puts his head in his hands. I can smell his deodorant mingled with boy's sweat.

"No one believes me," I say. I'm surprised at how shrill my voice sounds. I can't help it. I sound flustered, and I'm acting dumber than I am. I feel small and weak. I want him to take care of me.

"I believe you." He turns toward me. We look at each other. Someone else would kiss him now, but I'm frozen.

"Maybe I can get into her MacBook or phone," he says.

"How?"

"I just know how to do things."

I turn onto my stomach.

"Maybe she has everything in the cloud," he says. "Doesn't she have another computer? At work or something?"

I hadn't thought of that. "I think she always takes her MacBook with her."

"How do you know he goes by God?"

"Before her MacBook was erased, I saw a file titled 'God.' I was just barely able to mail it to myself. And there were two messages from someone called God on her phone. I also have a folder of hers that got locked for twenty-four hours because I entered the wrong password three times."

"Maybe those twenty-four hours are up?"

I spring up, grab my MacBook, and sit down next to Mees.

"I assume you tried all PIN codes and birthdates already?"

"Three, then it was locked."

He's sitting behind me now. "It's always a date that's easy to remember for whoever entered it. Try their wedding date."

I do. It doesn't work.

"Try and think of a code that's hard to guess for you but easy to remember for her."

"The date she and God met?"

"Can you find out when that was?"

"No. Let's try Grandpa's birthday."

I enter 11846. Wrong. One try left. The date he died? I can't remember it.

"Wait." I run downstairs. Grandma's in the large chair with Luuk on her lap. Her face is red and blotchy. They're looking through an old photo album.

"Look at this, sweetie," she says when she sees me. "Here's your mom, remember? In Italy, by Lake Garda. I think you were five, and Luuk was still a baby. It was so wonderful there. I went along to babysit you two so your mom and dad could go out for the night every now and then. I always thought they'd have another baby. I wanted more kids myself, did you know that?"

"Grandma, what's the date Grandpa committed suicide?"

"Good lord, child. Why do you ask that all of a sudden?"

"I was just wondering how old Mom was when it happened."

"It was in December. I found him in the early morning. On December 13, 1985. In the bath." She turns ashen. "Should we go for a walk with Chonk? We can use a bit of fresh air, guys. We're just sitting here . . ."

Luuk thinks it's a good idea and gets off Grandma's lap without letting go of her hand.

"Mees is upstairs, and he's catching me up on school and homework, so I'll skip it if that's alright."

The Grown-Up

She strokes my cheek and then grabs hold of my chin. "Oh, child, please don't get too caught up in the choices your grandpa and mother made. Please."

I want to comfort her. All of a sudden, I don't know what's worse for her: a daughter who chose to die or a daughter who was murdered. And which outcome is worse for me?

Back upstairs, I enter 121385

Bam—the folder opens.

An endless collection of photos. Breasts. Nipples. My mother's half-open mouth. Her ass. Mom on her hands and knees. A dick, no idea whose. A video. A balding head, the man licking her vagina. If people could die of shame, I'd already be dead.

Mees and I don't look at each other. He just says, "Holy crap." Then, after a really long silence, "You can't see his face."

"No," I say, "but you can see hers." Her body too, which I'd never associated with sex before. Her body, the source of my existence, and Luuk's. We used to cuddle up against it on the sofa. Those hands comforted our bodies, rubbed them with menthol cream when they were itching from chicken pox. Those arms sheltered us. Her body belonged to us, not to that man. I recognize the stretch marks on her stomach, those small, slightly sagging breasts, my thong on her ass, the gold chain with the little heart Dad gave her.

I slam my MacBook shut and want to throw it out the window. I never want to see or know about this ever again.

"You think that's the guy she was dating?"

"No, I think it's the mailman."

"You don't have to take it out on me, you know."

We're glued to the bed. Now what? How do you unsee something like this? I suspect Mees would like to leave, but he's afraid to. I've involved him in something he wants nothing to do with. My hands are sweaty as we sit there on the pink comforter, and the smell of soup is making me nauseous. I keep seeing it in my mind: Mom with her butt in the air, eyes half-closed.

"Hard to believe old people do that too," Mees says. And I know what he's thinking: *Not my mother. She's not this crazy.*

"Why not?" I say, more forcefully than I meant to. "They like sex too."

I begin to cry. Mees wraps his skinny arms around me. It would be wildly inappropriate to kiss him now.

"I won't tell anyone," he says. I'm draped against him like a wet rag. "Do you mind if I look again? Maybe there's a detail that can give us more information."

"No. If someone has to do that, I will." I free myself from the awkward embrace. "But you can help me set up a Tinder account."

He raises his hand, and I high-five him. "Great idea."

"We need pictures of someone like Mom."

"I have pictures of my mother."

"Oh my God, no. Imagine her boyfriend finding out."

"Then we'll just get some random photos, like half the people do on Tinder. Female, long hair, duckface, sunglasses on, feet on the edge of a swimming pool with a glass of wine. It doesn't really matter, does it? So long as we find him."

"And then we'll agree to meet up with him."

I don't know if I like it or think it's stupid that Mees is now involved all of a sudden. I basically friend-zoned him before this. I have a crush on him, but there doesn't seem to be any room for love on top of my sadness. I don't have the energy for that, and I feel guilty for even considering it. This time is about Mom, about finding out what actually happened. I want to get back to her, want to read on.

"You're tired, aren't you?" Mees says.

When I nod, he says in that case, he'll leave. He asks me to send some photos and tells me he'll set up the Tinder account tonight.

"Not together?" I say. I'm afraid he'll take control of everything, like boys do, unconsciously, but that's how they were raised. *Take control. Know-it-all.*

"I mean, you asked if I could help . . ."

The Grown-Up

"That's okay. It can't be that hard."

"You're weird."

He's right, I am weird. But it's confusing having him around. I'm acting more pathetic than I am. My voice is different, my body softer. My desire is making everything a blur.

"Sorry," I say again, and I kiss him on the mouth finally. No tongue.

18.

I'm meeting God tonight.

I know he's playing a tacky game, and if I were in a better space I'd probably think he was a total blowhard. He hasn't given me his real name, and even in his WhatsApp photo he covers his face with a hat. I haven't told anyone about our date because I'm in no mood for their concern, for being told I shouldn't trust him. I want a reason to crawl out of my brokenhearted despair and enjoy life again. I want to feel young, womanly, and desirable. God makes me feel all those things.

As I'm getting in the shower, he sends a message.

Should I pick you up? Looking forward to seeing you later X

Pick me up? At my house? Scary. But gallant too. And a bit awkward. He'll know my address. What if I open the door and he's disappointed? And why is this the first scenario that comes to my mind? He might disappoint me too. He could be a creep. I imagine myself opening the door, him pushing his way in and assaulting me in the hallway.

But if you let yourself be governed by fear, you're dead already. Didn't I say that to a client just yesterday?

I message that I'd like him to come get me and include my address.

You've just sent all your details to a man who doesn't reveal anything about himself, and you've invited him to your house.

But I have his number too.

The Grown-Up

Numbers don't mean anything anymore. SIM cards can be changed just like that. You're doing it all wrong.

I tell the voice in my head to leave me alone. I'll trust my intuition. If I don't feel right about him, I won't get in the car with him.

Who are you kidding? You'd get in the car with Ted Bundy. At least leave Kim his number or the address where you planned to meet.

Get a grip. It's only a date. I'll tell Kim if it turns into more than that. I'm in no mood for her questions: "Oh, you've gone out that much already? How was your first date? When's the guy after this? Why'd you choose the place tonight? Did you kiss him? Did he message you afterward? Do you feel butterflies? Will there be a second date?"

Kim's your friend. You don't want to tell her about this because you want to handle everything yourself, like always.

Kim's so critical. She always thinks she knows it all. I'm scared of her sometimes, just like those men who keep dumping her are.

How can you be so unkind about your best friend?

Kim and I are stuck together because of the men who left us. Peter took all the nice friends with him.

You're waiting until you've won this guy over to tell Kim because you want to show her up. You're quite mean to those few people who still want to be in your life.

I decide to view this as an exercise in trust and in letting go of fear. In the shower, I shave my armpits, my legs, my pubic area. Toward the end with Peter, I just let it grow, theoretically because I felt he should accept me as I am. Why should I make all the effort to keep our marriage going? But he no longer touched me, didn't see me anymore anyway. The one time I decided to shave completely and wait for him in bed in my red lace, he just laughed and said, "What are you doing?"

"Seducing you," I answered. Peter fled to the bathroom and said he couldn't do it like this, in such a contrived manner. It was the last time I'd let myself be rejected.

We never discussed it. I saw couples in my practice every day to whom I prescribed communication exercises. "When he's angry at you, try to imagine him as a child, a small boy, and feel yourself soften. And know this isn't about you. This is about old pain that the situation brings up again. Agree to continue the conversation the next day, over coffee, once the worst feelings of powerlessness subside. Never over drinks. Never at night. Never when you're short on time. Never with the children present. Never through other people."

Peter and I did all those things, all the time.

I turn my wet body in front of the mirror; hair shaved into a neat little landing strip, a small potbelly with stretch marks. Round hips, a fairly large ass (but that's the fashion now, says Lies), small, exhausted breasts that I'll have lifted and enlarged as soon as I can afford to, and shoulders proportionally a bit too narrow. I'm not beautiful, not ugly. I just am. Some would kill for a figure like mine, others eat just half a carrot every day just so they won't look like this. The question is: What does God see in me? I apply deodorant under my armpits and notice even these are starting to show wrinkles. If I don't stop looking at myself so critically, I'll wind up canceling our date and going back to crying and eating chips on the sofa. I'm fine. I look good. I'm a master at making big issues out of nothing.

What kind of impression do I want to make tonight? I stand in front of my clothes rack, over which I've haphazardly draped towels, sports clothes, and some old T-shirts repurposed as nightgowns. If only I'd known sooner he wanted to come get me. I'm looking through his eyes not just at myself now but at my house too. Eyes I don't even know yet, but which are finding fault already. Slovenly woman. Unhygienic. Disorganized. I've become a walking apology. *I'm not always like this,* I picture myself telling him. *You should see me when I'm with the kids.*

A hollow, nervous feeling takes hold of me. Does this mean he's the one, or the opposite? When I hear "The Day Before You Came" by ABBA come on the radio, I briefly take it as a sign. A sign! Ha ha, right. A sign that I have a wild imagination. It's a good thing I haven't told anyone about him yet. They'd laugh in my face.

The Grown-Up

Over my purple lace bra and panties, I wear my red silk hippie blouse with embroidered gold flowers that my mother gave me after a vacation to Ibiza. It's not real silk, but rather something synthetic that'll make me more likely to sweat, but it looks stunning on me. Underneath that, I wear flared, high-waist jeans that make me look slimmer, but which my heels often get caught in, especially on stairs, so I wear my Spanish boots too. I've had them for over twenty years, and now all of a sudden they're fashionable again. Being incapable of ever throwing anything away has its advantages. I hang some of Lies's gold chains around my neck, blow-dry my hair with the round brush, and go for a natural makeup look. Hippie chic. Clean face. Looking yourself by being yourself as little as possible. Not too eager, not too brazenly sexy, too desperate.

I go downstairs and wonder whether to put on my coat so we can leave immediately or light candles and pour wine. I choose the latter because it looks less desperate. I'm just at home, doing my thing, and I casually threw this on and was reading my book with a glass of wine. In moments like these, I wish I still smoked.

Seven o'clock. I pour my second glass of white wine. Do I have any nuts? Somewhere in the back of the cupboard, in the Christmas box Peter's office still keeps sending me for some reason. I put the bottle of sparkling wine in the refrigerator. In the hallway mirror, I see my hair has lost all its volume. *Cut it out with the whining already,* I hear Kim say. *Men think you're attractive. You look good, especially for your age. You know what's unattractive? Acting insecure. Chop chop. Tits out.* Is it normal for a person to have this many voices in their head?

I dawdle through the room, put on a random playlist, move cushions, pick up shoes that have been under the coffee table for three days, change the song, light a scented candle because all of a sudden I think it's smelly in here, while I tell myself it's completely normal to be fifteen minutes late. Rush hour, of course. I'm ashamed of all the thoughts I had. Where do I always get these illusions from? Hope? Why do I keep overthinking everything? I don't even want a relationship. I can't do that to my kids either. They've been through so much, been damaged so badly already. I consider cancelling our date. *Never mind, this is a mistake.*

Just as I'm pouring my third glass, the doorbell rings. I take a big gulp. He's twenty minutes late but surely has a good reason. I check myself in the mirror one last time, tell Chonk to shut up, and then open the door, probably grinning like a madwoman.

There he is, grinning too, wearing a black cap. Chonk barks and veers back.

"He won't do anything," I say, and then: "Hi, God."

"Godfried," he says, laughing, and kisses my left cheek.

We stand in the doorway together, sweat dripping down my sides. I feel small opposite his tall figure.

"I'm sorry I'm late. Traffic . . ."

"That's alright," I say. "Would you like to have some wine here first or leave right away?"

"My Uber's left already . . ."

"A glass of wine it is." I lead him into my house, into the living room. "Have a seat." I don't know why I sound so formal all of a sudden or why I'm feeling such tremendous fear. Maybe I'm confusing excitement and fear, but at least I'm feeling something, which I didn't have with the others.

He follows me into the kitchen. I can see the clutter through his eyes.

"Real cozy," he says, chuckling.

I get a glass from the cupboard. "Red or white?"

"I'll just have some water. I like to keep it as raw as possible."

"Raw?"

"Real. Straightforward. The naked truth. That's my resolution this year. No veiling anything."

"Interesting." I have some water too.

"You go ahead yourself, darling."

The Grown-Up

He's still wearing his cap. For the rest, he's wearing black sweatpants, Nikes, a white T-shirt, and a zippered black vest on top. He's wearing Beats earbuds around his neck, which I recognize because Lies really wants those. His teeth are almost too white. He chuckles again and starts to whistle when I look at him. He's odd. I'm still unsure if it's the cute type of odd.

"Jet," he says. He plops down on the worn-out Ikea armchair in the kitchen corner, drapes his legs across the armrest, and takes off his cap. Dark blond, medium-length hair, slightly thinning at the crown, hazel eyes, a neatly trimmed three-day beard. The way he moves reminds me of Mick Jagger. He pulls a cigarette from his pocket. "You're a psychologist."

"Yes." My mouth is dry. I take a sip of water.

"What do you think, is there such a thing as free will?" He puts the cigarette between his lips.

"Need a light?" I ask.

"No, I don't actually smoke. But back to my question, do we have free will?"

What an odd thing to ask.

"Yes, I think we do." I can't help but try to impress him with my knowledge. "We may be driven by unconscious intentions, by brain activity we're not aware of, but ultimately, provided we're in good mental health, we act consciously when we make decisions that might influence our lives or those of others. Even if those decisions also have to do with culture, our upbringing, peer groups, and all kinds of social structures."

"Interesting."

"I assume you don't drink out of free will, just like you won't light that cigarette out of free will."

"But the question is: Do you yourself drink out of free will? Did you invite me here out of free will?"

"There are all kinds of reasons why I'm having a glass of wine, and they don't all have to do with free will."

"Such as?"

"Nervousness. Habit. Addiction, perhaps."

He gets up, gives me a long look, and points at me while laughing boisterously. "Your face! I bet you're thinking: *What kind of lunatic did I let inside my home?*"

I'm uncomfortable and fascinated all at once. "We stopped using the word *lunatic* a long time ago," I tell him.

He comes nearer and gives me an amused look. "Come on, Twigs, let's go eat. Relax, that's it. Breathe in, breathe out." He puts his hands on my cheeks and blows on my face. His breath smells fresh. He gets his phone out to order an Uber. "Let's get out of here."

We drive into town. I still don't know his last name.

"Was that your dog?" he asks out of the blue.

"Yes. Chonk. I got him after Peter, my ex, moved out. Something to comfort the kids."

"And yourself, I assume, since you have free will."

"And myself. I wanted to shake things up a bit. To have a warm, living creature in the house when the kids aren't there."

"I hate pets."

There's a silence. *If a man doesn't like animals, he doesn't like people,* my mother always says about Peter.

God sits next to me with his eyes closed, his hands covering his mouth. I still don't know anything about him, other than that he doesn't believe in free will and hates animals.

"Where are we going, by the way?" I ask to fill the silence.

"It's a surprise."

He seemed childlike back at my house. Now he seems equally old and weary.

"Do you know how unusual it is that I got in a car with a total stranger without knowing where we're going?"

"You got in of your own free will."

The Uber stops at the Hotel Okura. God gets out, walks around the car, opens my door, and helps me get out. I've never felt such soft

The Grown-Up

hands. Hands that haven't worked a day, that have never been in hot dishwater or sanded a table. He draws me close, and I giggle, fake or sincerely I have no idea, but either way I'm impressed. The porter calls him "Mister Fred." The girls by the cloakroom simper about him. We step into an elevator, and he pushes the top button.

"The Okura bar. Nice, right?"

"Very nice." I can't afford a place like this, but I'm not going to start complaining. Before my divorce, I'd have picked up the tab so I'd look cool, but being such a spendthrift often has gotten me nowhere good. Plus these days my checking account is in the red three quarters of the month. Never divorce a lawyer. Better yet, don't ever marry one.

God orders a G&T with Hendrick's, Fever-Tree tonic, and cucumber. The barman appears to know him.

"I thought you wanted to keep things raw," I say.

He chuckles. "I changed my mind on the way here. Let's numb ourselves completely."

I get the feeling God will be pulling out all the stops to prove there's no such thing as free will. That's why I don't order the same thing as him but something complex from the menu, an old-fashioned.

"Well now, look who's being trendy."

When we get our drinks, we toast.

"To you, Jet . . ."

"Verschoor," I say.

"Nice to meet you. Godfried van der Duin." I make a note of his name. "Let the date begin."

The old-fashioned turns out to consist of straight whiskey with a dash of soda and orange peel.

"Stiff drink," God says.

I burst out laughing. "Sorry. I had no idea what an old-fashioned was, to be honest. It tastes as strong as if someone spiked it with something."

God laughs so hard other people stare at us. "That's terrible! Ha ha ha. I want one of those myself. Hugo, get me an old-fashioned. A spiked drink, I want it!"

I have tons of questions, but I don't get the chance to ask any of them.

"Listen, we've both heard other people's stories before. Kids, work, hobbies, divorce, dreams . . . As if anyone cares one bit what my hobbies are. Or what your kids look like. I don't have any kids. Someday, I'll want one. That's all well and good, but what I really want to know"— he taps his finger against my forehead—"is what's in that little head of yours. What makes you a good psychologist? I'm studying psychology myself, by the way."

"Online? One of your hobbies?"

"Tsk-tsk. No, officially: at the University of Amsterdam. I'm not even the oldest student there. But enough about that. What do you think of me? As a psychologist?"

I can't help but laugh. My jaws feel numb, and my tongue seems thick as a slug.

"Hugo," he says, "we'll have two more of these little numbers."

"No!" I cry, louder than I mean to. "Please, I'm foggy already. I'll just have a beer."

I look him right in the eyes. They look green now. One eye is smaller than the other. He smells of expensive aftershave, of wood and incense. I like that he's tall and has broad shoulders.

"As a psychologist, I never tell my clients what I think of them. I listen to them, observe them, and try to let them find the right answers themselves."

"But you do think something of them."

"Not always."

"Don't you write something in their file? What would you write in mine?"

"Come on, I only met you an hour ago!"

"That's exactly how long an intake interview takes. Tell me!"

"Look, I'm hungry, I've had one drink already, and I could only do that if you actually did an intake interview."

Once again, he lets out this weird, high-pitched laugh. "You're funny. You know that?"

I smile, because I'm a lot of things but funny isn't one of them. Or I should say, it's been quite a while since someone thought I was funny.

"Alright, Hugo, could we maybe get some sushi to eat at the bar here? Because what's happening here is magic. Listen, I'll just shut my fat mouth, and you're going to tell me what you'd write in my file. The red pill. No mercy."

"So this isn't a Tinder date but a therapy consultation?"

He gives me a straight-faced stare, then closes his eyes and makes a bring-it-on gesture.

"Hmm, let's see."

Hugo the barman puts a beer in front of me.

"This is off the record, and you can never use this against me."

He nods.

"Here's what I'd write: You like to unsettle. You like to deflect attention from yourself by clowning around. At the same time, you're preoccupied with what other people think of you, though I suspect you're not all that interested in others, personally. To you, other people are a means of getting to know more about yourself. It's hard to figure out what problem brought you into the intake because, though you're clearly looking for help, you're not giving away anything private. Maybe you're hoping to find someone to admire, who'll tell you what to do, like some kind of master. In this way, you're highly vulnerable and also complex. You want to both lead and be led. I hope you'll open up a bit more at your next appointment so I can help you."

I take a sip of beer. He sits motionless on the barstool, his eyes closed. "Holy fuck." He runs his hands over his head, trying to cover his bald crown with his thin hair. "You're good. By the way, I don't have psychological problems anymore, but you're actually talking about the person I used to be. I'm at my best now, though. I meditate, go to the gym, I'm studying, I read a book a week."

"I suspect you're often tired too."

"That's true."

"From trying to be perfect all the time. From trying so hard." A very easy diagnosis to make. Everyone will admit to being tired and trying hard.

A beautiful Japanese woman lays a large black plate of sushi in front of us.

"I don't know how I want you yet," he says. "As a psychologist or as a lover. Is both an option?"

I laugh because of how wildly inappropriate it is for him to say such a thing.

"Or are you offended now?"

I shake my head. I don't tell him that against my better judgment I find his blunt forwardness sexy, or that I feel alive for the first time in months, maybe even years. That for once I'm not thinking about my ex, my kids, my debts, my loneliness at all.

His body is some kind of magnet that's drawing me toward him, even though I know perfectly well I'm in danger. I know myself. Before I know it, I'll be at his feet and rolling myself out like a carpet, thanking him for trampling all over me.

"So you're looking for a therapist on Tinder?" I say.

God leans against the bar, head in hands, and laughs again. He picks up a piece of raw salmon with his other hand, dips it in the soy sauce, and sticks it in his mouth. He smacks his lips and then licks his fingers. He's like a ten-year-old.

"Provocative," I say. "I'd write that in your file too."

"My turn now," he says. "I think you're very sweet."

Right away, my eyes fill with tears, but I blink them away. It's been a long time since a man called me sweet.

"But beneath that, under that shield of sweet, you're furious. Right about here." He pushes his fingers against my midsection. "That's where it is. That's why you stoop forward when you sit, to contain all that anger. You seem quite relaxed, but inside that little head it's a tempest. It just goes on and on. All the time. *Did I do alright? Who'll screw me this time?* You're on guard. Disappointed. You think too much and feel too little. You're afraid your life is over. You desire but lack courage. You have a lot to offer, but you feel your life, your body, your femininity slipping away."

He talks in clichés. He's probably here every week, at this bar with Hugo as a sidekick, a different woman every time, but what he says hits home because it's true. God takes hold of my face and licks my tears. He's right: I'm alive, but dead already. I go through the motions because I love my children. When they're not with me, I'm in my tomb waiting for them to come back and breathe some air and warmth back into me. When they leave the house, I'm obliged to go on living for their sake. I see my future as a barren plain that I'm crossing all by myself, my only comfort the shadow of a grown-up child who comes to visit every now and then.

My eyes are burning from fatigue, but I don't want to stop reading. As long as I keep going, Mom's alive. I want to keep her with me for as long as possible. I'm crying, just like her. Crying for her loneliness and the pathetic way she clings on to this asshole. I hate having to read this, knowing she absolutely wouldn't want me to. Did she enjoy the secrecy, I wonder, or did she really not trust anyone around her anymore? Did she want to die? That's the question making the air in this house so oppressive I can hardly breathe. It's possible that one of us didn't want to go on living, and no one noticed. This Godfried's out of his mind, even a child could see that. Falling for his idiotic claptrap was a form of suicide too, just much slower than if she did it herself.

Maybe he's not an asshole, Lies. Did that ever occur to you? I can hear her say it. I wonder: What if she had introduced him to us at some point? But she didn't, and that's all I need to know.

19.

Waiting, that's what we're doing. In this bleak place that reeks of lilies and old flower water, with Chonk softly squealing all day, Luuk in front of the TV with his console, and Laura neurotically running around trying to make everyone happy. I heard her and Dad arguing again last night. Grandma checked into a nearby hotel because it didn't "feel right" to sleep at Dad's house with his new girlfriend. Her place has been taken over by Laura's mother, who's playing grandma as fanatically as Laura tries to play mom. "You're my bonus grandchild," she said as we were clearing the table. She wanted to pat me on the head, but I ducked away and told her I'm Lies, Jet's child and my actual Grandma's grandchild and nothing more.

We're waiting for Mom to be released so "we can bury her at last," as Dad put it last night. I think he's acting strange. We haven't yet decided whether to bury or cremate Mom, but I get sick to my stomach either way—at the thought of her body being lowered into a hole in the ground or put into an oven. Jochem's downstairs with a female police officer who introduced herself as Diewke. She looks like she could play on the Netherlands national women's soccer team with her fresh, makeup-free face and long blond ponytail. Jochem wants to speak with each of us privately, and he thought it best to come do this at our home. Informally, which might make it a little easier. He's set himself up in Dad's study. Dad always dreamt of having a room like this, but there wasn't any space in our old home. He jokingly calls it his man cave.

The Grown-Up

Dad thought it was absurd for Jochem to want to talk to Luuk and me, since we've been through so much already. Jochem said he understands, but that it's necessary since we were with her those last few days. Dad said he'd like to be present, then, too, but Jochem would rather he wasn't. Diewke will be there, and she specializes in children, How often do I need to say I'm no longer one of those? I want to be alone with Jochem because I think I can trust him. I also still think he's super handsome. He looks a bit like Mees, if he were older.

Jochem's waiting for me in the man cave while Diewke is with Luuk in his room. He's sitting in the chair Dad's so proud of, the Eames, and drinking a cappuccino. I want a cappuccino as well, and Laura brings me one. Her hands tremble as she puts down my cup on the glass coffee table, undoubtedly some fancy designer brand.

I was planning to tell Jochem everything I know because it's too much to hold in my head, but I'm afraid to now that I'm sitting here on the footstool opposite him. He's acting like he's just checking off the boxes, like he wants to be done with it already.

"Can you tell me one more time, in detail, how the day before your mother disappeared went?"

I take a sip and stare at the triangular meditation mat Dad brought back from Thailand, where he supposedly went to detox and destress. With Laura. There's a message in everything in this apartment, and it's *I've taken your mother's place.*

"Did you check all security cameras?" I say. "On this street or at the community of holiday cottages where you found her?"

"Of course. It's part of our job. The first thing we did. Only there aren't any cameras facing that street."

"But our neighbors across the street? Can't theirs see anything? Our front door, for example?"

"Their camera only shows people standing in front of their door. If no one's there, the camera doesn't record. As for the rest of the street . . . this isn't Amsterdam. Plus most of the houses are still under construction."

"And at the holiday cottages? There's a camera by the front entrance, isn't there? And a security guard?"

"There's a gate, which only opens with a pass. We found a pass for it in your mother's purse at home, so she didn't have it with her when she died. It's possible she got in by walking around the community's fence. The footage from that night shows several people approaching on foot, but they're quite difficult to recognize. Or I should say, you can hardly see them at all. The manager brags about the excellent security, but the system is actually quite old. The night footage is blurry, and honestly, so is the day footage for that matter. Plus, the wind caused one in ten security cameras to come falling down this season, including the one we're talking about now. So the video it took is pretty much useless."

"I'd recognize Mom anywhere."

"We really don't have anything, unfortunately. Just asphalt and a bunch of tree branches. No feet either. The only camera the wind didn't compromise is completely covered in pigeon shit."

"So my mother's murderer was able to walk in and out without anyone seeing?"

"And your mother too."

"So you have no idea how she got there?"

"Not by taxi or an Uber anyway. We've checked all that. We assume she arrived on foot."

Sparrenburg must be a two-hour walk from our place. A long walk, but a possible one.

I hold my head in my hands. Could God be so cunning to have known all about the messed-up cameras ahead of time? Had he decided it was the ideal place to take my mother's life? But why? From what Mom wrote, he seemed crazy about her.

"Alright, Lies, let's go over the day of her disappearance one more time."

What's the use? They already made up their mind how things went a long time ago. This conversation is pointless, but I dutifully do what he asks.

The Grown-Up

"It was just a normal day. She woke Luuk and me up for school. We took turns showering, and Mom made breakfast downstairs. I heard her sing along to a song on the radio, that song about a roller-coaster life. I got dressed, put on my makeup, and made my bed. I then went downstairs, where Luuk and Mom were at the table. They were teasing me because I was a bit moody that morning. 'Well, well, there's our teenager.' Luuk and I ate cornflakes. Mom was eating yogurt and granola. She'd prepared lunches for us."

My throat closes up. It's all coming back to me: Mom in her bathrobe, laughing and singing. She looked tired, scrawny, but she was acting cheerful. I want to go to her. So badly. It feels as if she's still just waiting around the corner for us to come home again.

"You're allowed to cry," Jochem says.

"Do you ever cry? I mean about your work, or during your work?"

"Yes," he says. "We're all only human, and it becomes a bit much for us sometimes too."

It sounds like something Mom would have said. It's odd to think she could be so wise sometimes and so unreasonable and angry at others. In my mind, I see the photos of her with that man again.

"Anyway. I biked along with Luuk to his school, then went on to the bus stop to go to my own."

"Did you notice anything about your mother that was different from other days?"

"No. Well, she was singing. And she messaged me. *I'm making lasagna tonight. I'm so happy you're my children, big kiss.*"

"Did she send such messages often?"

"She did right after Dad left."

All of a sudden, I'm afraid he'll see that message as confirming she committed suicide. I need to give him the story and photos. But I'm too embarrassed to do it. And what does any of it prove? Nothing. I'd be violating her privacy, and Jochem would only think my mother was a slut.

"And when you came home from school?"

"She got home later. I'd made tea already, and Luuk was at a friend's house. We had a chat at the dinner table. She'd brought brownies."

"What did you talk about?"

"I don't know, about school. And about Dad, how she was mad at him. He wanted to trade weeks during Christmas because he and Laura were going on vacation. She felt she'd traded often enough."

Jochem reaches for his cappuccino, and I do the same. We both take a sip at the same time.

"How did you feel about the fact that your parents kept arguing so much?"

"I thought it was stupid," I say. He keeps looking at me with those sweet eyes. Like the way Prince Harry looked at Meghan when they got married. Proud and supportive. That's the kind of man I want. "I'm not really sure what else I can tell you. They'd been separated for two years already. More than that."

"Did they argue this much when they were still together?"

"Toward the end they did. My mother pushed my father down the stairs once. Dad flung a teakettle at her head. One time, Mom got up and left the table while we were eating at Luuk's favorite restaurant for his birthday. I . . ." I can feel the blood rising to my cheeks. I'm about to say something I've never told anyone. "Once, during one of their arguments, I let myself fall through the glass coffee table just to make it stop. We had to go to the emergency room. All of a sudden, they were on the same side again, just parents instead of screaming head cases."

"I feel terrible for you. Two intelligent people who completely lose it like this."

I'm not sure if Jochem is allowed to say such things as a police officer.

He pulls a card from his inside pocket and hands it to me. "Here's my number and email address. Call if you need me, or if you just want to have a chat."

I take it. Is this a ploy? Does he really mean this?

"Anyway, so we had dinner together that evening, lasagna with salad, and then we watched *Temptation Island*."

"What time did you go to bed?"

"Luuk around half past nine. Me, an hour later."

"Did you go to sleep right away?"

"No. I went on Insta for a bit."

He doesn't need me to explain I mean Instagram. "Did you hear your mother leave?" he asks.

"No. I was wearing headphones."

He's writing something down in a notebook.

"I don't think my mother meant to leave. All her things were still at home. Her purse, her phone . . ."

"Maybe she did that on purpose."

"No way. She'd never just leave us by ourselves, and even—just suppose she really no longer wanted to live . . . She still wouldn't do it like this. Not with us at home, alone."

"Do you have any idea why someone would want to kill your mother?"

I hesitantly shake my head.

"You'd tell me if you did know something, wouldn't you?"

"Of course."

Don't do it, I tell myself. However sweet he seems. They'll rip it all from your hands or won't take you seriously. They'll see pornographic images of Mom. You're going to look for God yourself, and you're going to find him. Let him think he committed the perfect murder. Sneak up on him from behind.

"So your father and mother were arguing. Is it possible your father still came by later? To talk things over?"

I hold my breath. "My father can be rather mean to Mom, and she can be to him too. But he's no murderer."

"I'm not saying he is. But if your mother was murdered, it would likely have to be someone who knew her, and probably very well."

"Laura," I say, and I regret it immediately.

"How do you feel about her?"

"I hate her. Everything about her. Her mannerisms, her head, the way she touches my father, how she tries to be our mom, whoever she thinks she is. And especially when she starts crying and says things like 'I never wanted this, I never wanted to wreck your family.' *Oh, yes you did.* That's what I think then. *Stop lying. You wanted my father, and you were willing to sacrifice his family for it.*"

Jochem stares at his feet. An anxious feeling seizes me. Why's he so quiet all of a sudden? Why isn't he asking any more questions?

"Is something wrong?" I ask.

"No. I'm listening to everything you're saying and taking everything into account. The investigation is still open, but so far we don't have any leads that point to murder."

"What about that car, that black VW Golf that was parked in front of the door for some time?"

"We checked it all out. Turns out it was a Hertz rental car."

"Who rented it?"

"A man. He doesn't live in the Netherlands. He was lost, and he'd parked on your street to check Google Maps."

"That's a weird story."

"Perhaps, but there doesn't appear to be anything fishy about it. We have no reason to doubt the only evidence we have, which is your mother's note, handwritten, for heaven's sake."

Sweat is running down my back. More than anything, I wish I could throw myself in his arms and cry. Jochem is a real man. I know that I can't confide in him and that he doesn't believe me. But I feel sure he'd do anything in his power to help me.

He extends his hand and gives me an encouraging smile. I'm not a woman to him but a child he feels sorry for. "I promise I'll keep my mind open to other scenarios if you promise to call me if you think of something I should know."

I shake his hand and lie, looking him straight in his pale blue eyes.

The Grown-Up

"Godfried van der Duin," I type in the Google search bar. No results there, nor on Facebook or Instagram. God doesn't appear to exist, nor does a Fred van der Duin. Still, he was with my mother at the Okura bar, where everyone knew him. I need to go there, but first I need to make a Tinder profile. Apparently you only need a phone number for that. I sign up, receive a verification code, and just like that I'm in. Now to think of a name. What are women Mom's age called? Marieke, Annelies, Marjon. Only, the type God is looking for has a different name. Fleur, for instance.

I keep typing: Fleur is forty-two, recently divorced, works as a psychologist, and is looking for a mate. *Upload your profile photo,* Tinder instructs. I search Google for a Fleur who's a psychologist. I find a pretty, friendly-looking woman of around forty with thick blond hair and soft blue eyes. And with a Facebook account. I lift three nice, but also somewhat blurry, photos from her album. One in the snow, where she's wearing a red ski jacket, a white hat, and sunglasses, and one where she's on a boat with a broad smile, hair blowing in the wind, a glass of wine in hand. It's amazing how easy this is.

Could God be so crazy as to go back on Tinder right after he murdered my mother? And would he like someone like Fleur next? He's crazy alright. I read all about that in Mom's document. And he's obsessed with psychology. Now I just need to find him among all those thousands of men. I've only seen his dick and his balding crown between my mother's legs. Maybe his rotten face is recognizable in one of those disgusting photos.

I open the folder. I briefly stare at the first photo of Mom like I don't know her: naked in bed, a rose between her breasts, shooting a semi-seductive glance to the camera.

I feel her presence. Like she's still alive and might walk into my room at any moment and fly into a temper. *What are you looking at, dammit?* I'm so mad at her. But I miss her even more than I'm mad. How the hell am I going to live without her? With Dad and that fucking Laura? Get a degree, move into a house with someone, marry, have babies?

I wipe my tears with my fist and skim the photos as fast as I can. It appears God put some thought into this: he never photographed or sent anything that showed his face. I watch the videos, focusing on anything but their genitalia. I see a bookshelf against a white wall with a painting of some kind of sunset beside it. I pause the video and take a photo with my phone. This isn't her bedroom. Another video. His chest, which he appears to shave. A wrist with a woven leather armband, a silver clasp. "Don't film me!" he says. Mom's nervous giggling. He tries to take the phone from her, and she cries, "No." And then, in a flash, his face.

I pause the video again. His mid-length hair hangs down his face. He's grinning, but his eyes are furious. He has an unusual nose, a bit of a knob. The scene was filmed from below—no idea if I'd be able to recognize him from this.

I press play again. It looks like the phone falls from Mom's hand onto the ground next to the bed. All I can hear is them laughing and moaning, and then he says, "You like that, don't you?" followed by a long silence. The phone is on the floor but continues to record. The ceiling. A paper lamp like we have at home too. Ikea, €7.99.

"Don't ever film me again. Say it."

What are they doing? Some kind of S&M?

"I'll never do it again." Mom's voice is pinched.

"Sweet good girl." Then the recording stops.

20.

"I'll book us a room," he says. We're having coffee with cognac. We're the only ones left in the bar. "Because I think Hugo wants to go home too."

It's half past one. It feels like only five minutes since we got here. My palms are getting sweaty. I need to call a taxi, but I don't have any cash with me, and I don't want him paying for everything.

"You're coming with me," he says. He grabs my chin and kisses me. I haven't kissed like this in years. Perhaps I never have. Deep, forceful, and soft at the same time, desirous and wet.

"I'll decide that for myself, thank you."

"Decide all you want. The tab's been paid. If you want I'll order an Uber for you."

"I have a dog at home that needs to be walked."

"Do you know who needs to be walked? You."

The room is enormous. Beige carpets, beige chairs, beige curtains. God lets himself fall onto the caramel-colored bedspread. He holds his hands under his head and looks at me. His stomach is strikingly white.

"Come here," he commands, and it seems him ordering me about is fine with me. More than fine, it turns me on. I don't like having to choose, to doubt, think, or decide. *Come.*

I sit down beside him. You can see the entire city from the giant window next to the bed. He's running his hand over my back. I'm about to have sex, and I'm so caught up in my thoughts that I'm no longer sure whether I actually want to. He'll devour me, but there's no going back now.

His hand strokes my hair, folds around my neck, and he pulls me toward him, sticks his tongue in my ear. His breath smells of coffee and alcohol.

There's a knock at the door. Godfried springs up and opens it. A waiter wheels in a cart with a champagne cooler on it.

"Thanks, friend." He pulls a 50-euro bill from his pocket and gives it to the waiter.

"Would you like me to open the bottle for you?" the waiter asks before he leaves.

"Oh no, we can do that ourselves."

God casually uncorks the bottle and pours two glasses.

"Do you feel safe?" he asks. Now he's the one playing therapist.

"Honestly, no. I feel safe when I'm on my sofa with Chonk on my lap, a cup of tea, Netflix on, and the kids in bed upstairs. But is it a good sign to 'feel safe' on a first date, or the opposite? It might be boring if I felt safe."

"There's Miss Rationality again." He hands me my glass. "Are you thinking, *Maybe he slipped something in it?*"

"I wasn't," I say. "But now I am." I take a sip.

He then does the same, leans in toward me, and presses his mouth against mine. He lets the champagne run out. I get the feeling everything's a test with him.

He takes the glass from my hand and pushes me back onto the bed. He undoes my belt, lowers the zipper of my jeans, takes off my boots and socks, and pulls down my pants and then tosses them on the beige chair.

"Spread your legs."

I do it.

"Wider. Your knees too . . . Yeah, like that." He looks down at me, standing between my legs, a glass of champagne in hand. "Beautiful," he says. "My own hot little psychologist."

The Grown-Up

I've never yearned to be touched as much as I do right now. I'm reminded of what a tarot card reader once told me: *You have to surrender yourself, naked like a baby.* That was about my marriage at the time, which was heading for a cliff. Only lying here now, though, do I really know what surrender means. He could murder me if he wants, degrade me, rape me. If this isn't surrender, I don't know what is. He stoops down and takes off my panties, then studies my vulva. I don't know him. I don't know what he's doing. Maybe I'm in danger. I'm a mother. Mothers don't do things like this. I close my eyes, try not to think about how I'm lying here, about his eyes on my tattered body. Two children came out there. I had to be cut with scissors for the first. You can still see the scar, a line toward my right thigh. He traces it with his finger. Then finally he fully presses his mouth to me and licks me like I'm his favorite ice cream flavor.

When the shame becomes too much, I pull him up and kiss him. He unbuttons his pants, kicks them off, dropping his champagne glass in the process.

"Look at me," he says, and I know I'm lost. His eyes, sometimes green, sometimes gray, sometimes blue, his gaze, fierce and serious. At last, just like that, the moment arrives: after two years of yearning, after Peter rejected me so many times I worried no one would ever find me desirable again. Here it is, the sex I needed so badly, according to Kim. And what sex it is. I almost feel like taking a photo of God's penis and sending it to Peter: *And you thought* you *were something . . .*

There's nothing soft, sweet, or timid about it. God's taking me, and I'm surrendering. He's maintaining full control.

"I'm coming," he says. "Look at me." I turn my head as far as I can. I look at him through my sweaty hair, and he looks back at me, sternly. I'll never forget this image. We stare at one another as our bodies pump together. His mouth is half-open, his eyes squinting, his jaw tense. He comes and then collapses on top of me.

It's four o'clock, and we're drinking champagne again. My self-loathing is back. I'm such a slut. Leaving the dog by himself this long, for sex. God's already talking about whether the difference between men and women is a matter of nature or nurture—as far as he's concerned, it's obviously nature, and he has a thousand theories to back this up. I listen, but without hearing anything. I'm lying with my head on a naked man's chest. I can hear a heartbeat. I'm with a human being. I didn't think this would ever happen again. Despite this, I say: "I need to leave."

"I'll be gone tomorrow," he says. "So enjoy it while it lasts." He kisses me like he's saying goodbye already.

"Where are you going?"

"On the road."

I get up to put on my clothes.

"Don't you want to take a shower?"

"I'll do that at home."

"Come on, Twigs, hang around for a bit."

"Twigs?"

"That's my name for you."

"Why?"

"Because you are like a twig. Like a small stick. Unbending. Rigid. Thin."

"I'm not thin."

"Yes you are. I can see right through you. You're translucent, like tissue paper."

My head fills with a dense fog. I'm no longer able to think or feel, disappearing beneath his words.

"Does that offend you?"

I shake my head and pretend to laugh, then put my feet in my jeans and almost fall over.

"Well now, madam appears to be in a hurry to leave all of a sudden."

"I need to get back to my dog."

"You don't need to defend your reasons, Twigs. You're free to go. You have free will."

Bra on, blouse over my head. I want to both stay and run away.

"Anyway," he says, "I had a great evening. With you."

The Grown-Up

"Me too. Thanks for everything. You should know, by the way: I don't normally let a man pay for everything."

"I know everything already, Twigs."

I go to the bathroom so I can use the toilet and brush my teeth. All his things are lined up neatly. Two toothbrushes, toothpaste, an entire row of pill bottles, expensive cologne, even more expensive body lotion. There's a label from an American pharmacy on one of the bottles. Oxycodone. The next jar contains clonazepam, the third dihydrotestosterone.

"I travel a lot, so that's what I have the clonazepam for, and the oxy's for my hernia. What you're holding there is for my hair, in hopes I won't start looking like my father, who's as bald as a cue ball."

He stands behind me, still naked, and puts his arms around my waist. He unfastens my belt, pulls my jeans down, and bends me over the washbasin. "Pretty flexible for a Twigs," he says. He takes me with short, hard thrusts as we stare at each other in the mirror. Within just a few minutes, he comes. "See, there's nothing wrong with my potency."

I walk to the toilet with my pants still around my knees and relieve myself.

"As you've probably guessed, I've been sleeping here already, for a week now. I just love hotels, the anonymity."

"Why'd you lie about it?"

"Trying to act cool?"

He reminds me of Luuk, when I catch him on the step stool trying to help himself to the sweets I keep in a tin on top of the refrigerator.

"It makes no difference to me," I say. "We're not in a relationship. But since I've been cheated on before: Do you have a girlfriend?" I point at the toothbrushes.

"That's for if someone comes to spend the night. You, for instance."

I wipe myself, pull my pants back up, and flush. Then I wash my hands as calmly as I can. My heart has turned into a chunk of stone. *Save yourself,* I think.

"Your Uber's here," he says.

All the intimacy from a few minutes ago seems to have evaporated. We embrace like strangers at an AA meeting.

"Like I said, I'll be gone tomorrow. God's going to America." He chuckles about this himself. "It's a pretty stupid name, Godfried, don't you think so?"

I'm afraid to answer. Maybe it's another test.

"It means 'living under God's protection.' But my parents named me after the novelist Godfried Bomans. At least, my mother did. My father didn't have much of a say."

It seems he's starting a whole new story, but I need to leave. I can hardly muster the attention he demands anymore.

"Enjoy your trip," I say. "Let me know if you need me."

"I don't have a return ticket yet," he says. And then: "Come to New York."

I blow him a kiss as I walk away. I want to run. I hear the door behind me open again.

"Twigs, look!"

I turn. He's naked in the hallway, waving his dick around.

I make coffee when I get home. I don't want to shower yet so I can enjoy our smell for as long as possible. It's the first time in two years that the emptiness of my house doesn't descend on me like a wet blanket. I sit down at the kitchen table. My hands are shaking as I bring the coffee to my mouth. Why did I feel I needed to get away from him? There's nothing I'd like more than to go back now, to get in bed with him and do it another thousand times. I reach around in my purse, looking for my phone. Maybe he sent me a message. The phone isn't there. I go to the hallway and go through my coat pockets. Not there either. I didn't leave it in the Uber, did I?

In this moment, my phone is my crystal meth, my only direct line to him. I get my MacBook and google "Find My iPhone." I type my phone number and Apple ID. Entering the verification code takes a little while, but then a map of the area appears. My iPhone is marked by a blue dot somewhere on the A4 motorway—it's in the Uber. I stare

The Grown-Up

at the screen, wondering what to do. I don't have the driver's details and no phone to call him.

The blue dot is heading toward me. Did the driver find it, and is he doubling back now? Hallelujah!

I keep my eyes glued to the screen like a fan watching the extra time in a soccer final. My phone exits onto Anderlechtlaan, then continues down De Alpen onto Inaristraat: my crystal meth is on its way to its user.

I jump up when the doorbell rings and run to answer it. And then, there he is, with a huge grin, wearing jeans and a spotless white fitted shirt. He dangles my phone in front of my face like a carrot.

"You forgot this, Twigs."

When did Mom change? Did I see or notice anything? Were we all so caught up in ourselves? I can't think of anything. Luuk and I went to Dad's every Monday. He would pick Luuk up from school, I would ride my bike over to his shitty place, and Mom would leave our bags with the receptionist at Dad's work. The transition went as smoothly as everyone could make it. Whatever clashes they had now were limited to their WhatsApp conversations.

In the beginning, Luuk and I would wonder what Mom was doing when we weren't there. Whether she was lonely. If she cried. We were certainly lonely ourselves at the kitchen island during the evenings, with Dad fuming on his phone and Laura playing stepmother of the year. Grown-ups can act so fake.

"You can tell us anything. We both love you just as much."

"But do you still love each other?"

"In a different way."

"What kind of way?"

"More as fellow parents."

"What does that mean?"

"That we respect each other."

They hated each other.

21.

It's my first day of school since Mom went missing. Classmates hug me, and teachers look at me longer than usual. No one has the nerve to ask anything. A mother who kills herself is very different from a mom who dies from a terminal illness. Maybe it would be better to believe in her suicide like Dad does. To believe it was her choice. *It's very sad, but at least she isn't suffering anymore.* That's how people try to comfort me. It's sickening to think a mother would rather be dead than with her children. It's also sickening to think Mom left us at home alone to go fuck some crazy man. Parents tell you they love you unconditionally, but they don't. Not unconditionally enough to keep you out of their love life. Though Mom actually did manage that much while she was alive. Dad didn't. He just had to start all over again. A new place and family, with us two kids moved over like a couple of figurines.

Mees and I sit on the fence by the bicycle shelter. I show him the Tinder profile. His head is so close to mine I can smell his hair. The smell reminds me of hay.

"So let's get swiping," he says.

I click the flame icon. A muscular man in a red bathing suit appears. Michel's thirty-five and nine miles away. I swipe left, and then Richard appears. He's old. Forty-nine, he writes, but I think he's lying. Thin gray hair, a childish Superdry T-shirt. He looks angry.

"How does a man like that think anyone will like him?" Mees asks.

"I'm sure there are older women who are desperate."

The Grown-Up

Single, open to adventure. No ONS but MNS.
"What are ONS and MNS?"
I have no idea. "Doesn't matter, let's keep looking."

We swipe our way through hordes of balding men in black sunglasses, on bicycles, on boats, on motorcycles, on sofas, laughing men with beards behind barbecues, next to cars and blurred-out women, flexing their muscles at the beach, their six-packs, anonymous individuals who think they're funny with their pictures of frogs, or inspiring with some spiritual quote. There are couples looking to hook up together with a third, married men looking for a fling, the occasional individual wanting to make friends.

"Those really good-looking guys, are they some sort of prostitutes?" Mees asks. As if I know about such things.

"No idea."

"Like one, just to see."

"We're looking for God."

"Do you think he still calls himself God?"

"No. I think if he's still on here, or on here again, he'll be going by something like Fred, or Duin, or Dune, and then have a picture of himself with a hat, or of a ferret, or something with some quote. He thinks he's smart."

We keep swiping. "You're going too fast," Mees says. "I think I saw Mr. Van Dam." Our math teacher. "Isn't that hilarious? Like him!"

I try to close myself off from Mees's stupid comments. God's lurking somewhere alongside all these desperate guys. Prowling, hunting for some lonely woman. I hope I made Fleur look like ideal prey. Pretty, but not implausibly so, her desperation covered with a considerable veneer of toughness. Mother to a child. A psychologist.

I stop swiping at a photo of a sleeping man wearing a white hat with a black band over his face. A three-day beard.

"Thinking is shallow, feeling brings you closer to your soul," it says.

"That's him," I say.

"How do you know?"

He did the same thing in his other profile. A hat in front of his face. The man calls himself Nude and is forty-nine years old. But it's the line below it that clinches it. *Plays Tinder on level 9.* I'm sure now.

"Nude," I say. "Like *Dune* with the letters switched around. And then that phrase about thinking and feeling. He said something like that to Mom. *Don't think. Feel!* He was wearing a white suit in his previous profile photo too, with a hat covering his face. It's definitely him."

I swipe right, and the jubilant words appear: "It's a match!"

"Oh my God," Mees sputters.

"In the flesh."

"So now what?"

"Wait until he sends something."

Mees grabs my arm and then my shoulder. He wants to act happy, but he can't quite do it. My mother's still dead.

Back home after school, Laura, Grandma, and Dad are waiting for Luuk and me. All three have red, blotchy faces. I wonder what kinds of dramas are unfolding here when I'm not home. Grandma, unwaveringly stubborn; Laura, whose life is completely consumed by our dysfunctional family; and Dad, wallowing in guilt and anger.

"Hey, guys," he says.

"How come you never say, *Hey, girls?*" I ask.

Laura laughs a nervous, high-pitched laugh but stops immediately when she catches Dad's glance.

"Listen," Dad says and pulls Luuk close. I take off my backpack. My stomach is growling. Grandma makes tea. I've had it up to here with tea, with everything and everyone. "Mom's body will be released tomorrow."

He's silent for a while. That combination of words: *Mom* and *body*. I can't accept this. If I were smaller, I'd stick my fingers in my ears, like Luuk's doing now.

"Sweetie, I know it's really sad."

The Grown-Up

Luuk kicks Dad in the shin and starts crying like he's only three years old, then runs upstairs.

"Let me," Grandma says, and she goes after him.

"So?" I say. I avoid looking Laura or my father in the eye.

"We can bury her."

"So?" I say again, with more emphasis.

"The police are closing the dossier," Laura says. The hand she uses to give me a cup of tea is trembling.

I feel like I'm going to be sick.

"We have to accept it, sweet Lies," Dad says.

"I don't have to do a fucking thing." I don't say it very loud, but Laura looks startled.

"I understand you're angry, but I'm not used to hearing such language from you. That's not how we speak to one another." Dad goes over to Laura and puts his arm around her.

"'We.' There is no *we*. There's you two, and there's Luuk and me. 'We'? That was with Mom."

I look at the kitchen counter with nothing on it except for an enormous, shiny espresso machine. They took a barista course together. When I told Mom, I thought she'd die laughing.

"It's okay, sweetie. I understand, and I'll give you room to be as angry as you want. I'll keep loving you no matter what."

"Who taught you to talk like this? Your therapist?"

"Your father's doing his best, Lies. We're all doing what we can," Laura says.

I feel like smashing everything on the table.

"Either way," Dad says, rubbing his eyes, "Grandma was there this morning, and we've decided not to have an open casket and to bury her at Zorgvlied."

"So I'll never see her again?"

"The coffin will be closed during the wake."

"Would you like to see her one last time?" Laura asks. Dad sighs. I get the feeling he's told her to stay out of it.

"I don't know . . . Maybe I do." My stomach turns at the thought of seeing her like that, but it'd be worse to never see her again.

"If that's what Lies wants, you'll need to take care of that, Peter."

Dad looks like he's about to break down any moment. "I can't, Laura."

It's generally a bad sign when grown-ups start addressing each other by their first names.

"You need to take their wishes into account."

I get the feeling that she wants to tell him something completely different, that saying this is a way for her to bring up her own wishes.

I take a sip of tea. Mom's dead. She'll be buried. Our lives will go on, when in fact everything should come to a stop. "But suppose she was murdered . . ."

"She wasn't murdered, Lies," Dad says.

"Does the idea that she was murdered make you feel better?" Laura's stepping into her self-assigned role as therapist.

"I'm sure of it," I say. "It's also rather convenient for you two to think she was unhappy enough to do something like that. And for the police too. It's not convenient for us, Dad. Not for Luuk and me. I know you hate her, but we know better. She was a great mom. She would never do this."

Dad begins to sob. "Lies, can't you see how difficult this is for me? I left her, and she ends her life . . . Don't you see this was my worst fear? And that I'll have to live with this now? What if I hadn't left her?"

"She'd still be alive." One at a time, I look Laura and Dad straight in the eye. I want to see them wither away. "Go ahead and cry," I say. "You two wanted to live together in this mausoleum so badly. Well, here we are. Isn't this fun?" I'm talking in Mom's voice, saying things she might say.

Laura turns around, grabs her purse from the tall chair, and walks off unsteadily.

"Enough!" Dad shouts, just like he used to shout at Mom.

The Grown-Up

I throw my hands in the air. "What can I say? The truth's fucked up, Dad."

I run up the stairs past Grandma. She tries to stop me, but I push past her. "Lies!" She calls after me. "That's no way to talk to your father!"

I lock my door behind me. My anger has nowhere to go. It surges through my body. I feel like breaking something, and at the same time I feel guilty about what I said to Dad. It's all intertwined. I'm angry at him, angrier than I've ever been at anyone, but I also want to cry against his chest. And I want him to understand me. To take me seriously. I may be his daughter, but I'm not a child anymore.

22.

I lie awake beside a softly snoring man. When he sleeps, he's like a giant baby, the way he keeps his fist by his mouth. The second man in two years. There was that time with Jan, my colleague, but that was a slipup, like the one time with Peter when I'd just bought this bed and assembled it myself, after an emotionally draining move. The kids were with him and Laura; Mom and Kim had just left. It was the first evening in my new house, in the newly built neighborhood I didn't want to live in, by myself, which I didn't want to be. I drank a bottle of wine and was just about to go to bed when the doorbell rang. Peter was a bit tipsy. It was Friday, and he'd come straight from café De Blauwe Engel. We hadn't seen each other in months and only talked through our lawyers. Which, for the record, had been my decision. My lawyer said I needed to detach from him, put my emotions aside, and fight for what was mine. Peter wanted to stay friends and do family things together, which drew ridicule from my lawyer. "Ha ha, yeah, right. Stay friends. That'll save him a lot of money, and he'll be able to depend on you as he sees fit." We went for a clean break. Being friends and divorcing didn't mix.

But here he was, babbling half-drunk about how awful he felt for me, asking whether I was doing alright in my new house. Then all of a sudden, he began to cry. "Don't think I don't miss you. Our family. You're still the love of my life."

The Grown-Up

I was too dumbfounded to be angry, and I felt moved. I also realized this was my opportunity to hurt Laura, so I offered him a glass of wine and gave him a tour of the house. In the bedroom, still bare and filled with boxes, I put my arms around him. We had a quick fuck. He must have told me how much he missed my ass at least twenty times. After he'd come, I asked him to leave. I hoped he would refuse, but he said: *Yes, that's probably best. Sorry. I wish everything was different.*

That night, I lay as wide awake as I am now. A thousand thoughts. A new man in my life, just like that. One minute I'm thrilled about it, then the next I'm terrified, and then I'm angry with myself for getting so carried away. He calls me Twigs, which isn't a nice nickname at all. He's arrogant and like a three-year-old at the same time. And how is he combining his psychology studies with traveling the world? In any case, he's managed to get inside my head. If I was talking to one of my clients, I'd say, *You let him in to take your mind off yourself.*

His phone on my nightstand lights up constantly. When I flip it over, I see a long list of WhatsApp messages. I don't read them. No doubt I'm not his only fling.

"Sneak a peek?"

I'm startled and turn toward him. "I couldn't sleep because it kept lighting up."

"Should we have a look together?"

"I'd rather not."

"Come on, don't you want to know what's on my phone?" He reaches over me and gets it from the nightstand.

"I really don't."

"It's alright, dear. I went through your phone too."

"How?"

"Birthdate PIN code. Easy."

"How'd you get that?"

"Facebook. Yep, that's what all you woman share with Marky Zuckerberg and the rest of the world."

"I find this highly inappropriate."

"I find this highly inappropriate," he repeats after me, mocking me, then grins and gives me a long kiss. "That's why I'm not on there."

"But you are, or else you wouldn't be able to see my Facebook profile."

"Everyone can see your Facebook profile. It's set to public. You need to change that." He puts his arm around me and holds me close. "Sweet Twigs." He smells my hair. "Look," he says, holding his phone in front of my nose. "This here's Anouk. A model. Looker, isn't she?"

I freeze up. He's insane.

"I could be with her if I wanted, but I'm with you. You're Champions League." He taps his finger against my head. "Smart chick. So this one . . ." He zooms in on the photo of Anouk, who's exceptionally beautiful indeed: long, dark blond hair, perfect teeth, narrow shoulders. "We'll just quickly delete her. Bye bye, Anouk." He clicks a button, then tosses his phone beside the bed and pulls me up on top of him. He takes my face in both hands. "Don't take everything so seriously."

Minutes later, he's inside me.

"You see right through me," he says, and it's a lie, but I choose to believe him.

The following day, I'm sore all over. I go out to walk Chonk without showering first. My cheeks and chin feel like they're on fire from all the kissing, I'm sore in between my legs, and my whole body is tingling. I'll keep my distance after this. *He's toxic*, I'd tell a client. It feels as if he's turning me into a zombie. But still, I find myself singing, I go the whole day without eating, I pick up my kids from school whistling. I even wave at Laura.

These mixed feelings persist over the following weeks. Kim thinks it's very strange. A man who goes through my phone, who calls me Twigs, who seems to have ghosted me, who showed me pictures of other women.

"Come on, Jet, you're a psychologist, for crying out loud. Time to be done with this. You had a good time, he gave you your spark back. Use those pheromones and go out and date or fuck anyone you want.

The Grown-Up

But this guy sounds like bad news. I'd block him. You've only just gotten out of your slump, and this guy's sure to pull you back down, and deep too."

I say she's right and delete his number from my phone. *Block him*, she says. *I will*, I say. Only, I just happen to forget. I google him and search on Tinder but don't find anything. I even go to the Okura bar for cocktails with a colleague. Hugo the bartender doesn't recognize me.

I've nearly forgotten him altogether when my phone rings one night. It's eleven o'clock, I'm just going to bed. Lies is down for the night already, staring at her phone.

"Twigs," and then his little laugh. "How's life?"

My chest contracts. "Good," I say. I flee to the bathroom and lock the door.

"Listen, beautiful. I'm in London. And I was thinking: maybe Jet feels like dropping by. Because I had a great time with you."

"Yeah," I say.

"So you'll come?"

"No, I mean I had a good time too. But I can't come to London just like that. I have my kids. Work . . ."

"Are you playing hard to get?"

I laugh. "I haven't heard from you in two months. That's what I'd call playing hard to get."

"Sorry. I had business to tend to. Needed some R & R too. Because I thought it was quite something, my time with you. And I don't really want that. I'm a wolf who needs to roam. But there's not much wandering left in me, I can tell you."

Lies is fumbling with the door. "Mom? What's the matter?"

"Nothing," I say, covering the phone with my hand. "A client. Go back to sleep.

"Can I think about it first?" I ask.

He bursts out laughing. "Don't think too long. I want to see you."

"Alright. I need to check up on my kids now."

"You need to think about yourself more."

"Good night."

"Do you want to see me too?"

I'd like to roll myself out naked on the spot for him.

"I'll let you know. I need to go now."

That laugh again. "Bye, beautiful."

The next morning, an enormous bouquet of flowers is delivered to my practice. I never gave him the address, but of course it's not too hard to find.

"Dear Twigs, I hope you'll come. Don't think about it, trust your feelings."

I take off the card before my colleagues see it.

I'm writing all this down because I want to understand myself better. How it got to this point. How I stepped into every possible pitfall. Understanding myself will allow me to help my clients better. Why did I ignore every red flag? I want out of these toxic games, of craving his validation.

I've stopped talking to Kim about it. She thinks it's over with him. No one knows anything. That's probably a bad sign. I keep the trip to myself, convince myself it's something private, just for me. A goodbye outing. After this, it'll be over. I decide to say I'm going to an EMDR conference in Innsbruck that really is taking place that weekend, exactly during the week Peter has the kids.

The same evening I find my boarding pass in my mailbox, he also sends me a video of his penis, hard, along with a message:

We can't wait.

23.

When I go back downstairs, the three grown-ups fall silent. Gauging by the tension in the room, they seem to be in disagreement over something.

"Lies, dear, what are you doing?" Grandma asks.

"Going for a bike ride," I say.

"Well, we were just talking about it, and if you'd really like to see your mom one more time, I'll join you," she says. "Perhaps Luuk wants to go too."

Laura lays her hand on top of Dad's.

"Okay," I say. I need to be strong now.

"But if we're going, we need to go now."

"Why?"

"I was with her this morning. We made her look very beautiful. I put that new dress on her, remember? The green one with little gold moons. We washed her and did her makeup . . ."

I don't understand how she can talk like this is a normal thing to do.

"The coffin will be closed tomorrow," she says.

"Shouldn't you go too?" Laura asks Dad.

"No," I say. "I don't think Mom would want that, and neither do I, to be honest."

"That's quite a hurtful thing to say to me, Lies."

Laura grabs him by the arm again.

"But it's true," I say.

"Shall we call Luuk? Ask if he wants to come along?" Grandma's in full de-escalation mode.

"I'll go get him," I say. As I walk away, I hear Grandma say this will be good for us and help us process everything.

"They've been traumatized enough already, Tineke. I don't think I can support this, I really don't."

"We'll all be together. We'll form a ring of love around them."

"Lies just accused me of murdering her mother!" Dad cries. "So much for your 'ring of love.'"

"Do you want to know how long Jet held me responsible for her father's suicide? It's normal, it's part of their process. Their helpless rage has to be directed at something. Better you than themselves."

"Well, great. But Jet's the one who did herself in."

"Yes. And you and I are both to blame for that. We lost sight of her. We won't let that happen to the kids. And that's why you're coming with us."

Dad holds Luuk's hand. We're walking down a gravel path toward some kind of chalet with a red roof and black siding.

"It's beautiful here, isn't it?" Grandma says. "Can you hear the birds? So peaceful." She's acting as cheery as possible. I don't understand how she does it. Her child's here. Dead.

Luuk's dragging his feet like he's a toddler again, holding on to Dad's hand with both of his. In my mind, none of this is real yet, and Mom just took a secret trip to London with God. At least she lives on in her story. In it, she has a secret, like I have a secret now.

Grandma has the key to a room in the mortuary. "We're allowed to see her the rest of the day and tonight. If you want, you can write or draw something inside the coffin." She's rambling.

"It smells funny in here," Luuk says. He stays by the door. I watch Dad turn gray and hard, like stone. Grandma walks over to the coffin of blond wood, stoops over it, and begins to talk. "Hey, sweetie. Your kids are here. They're a bit frightened, but you look beautiful. Come, guys. Come sit with your mom for a bit." Grandma's either lost her mind or she's medicated. I slowly walk up to join her. Luuk stays by the door, his hands under his armpits. Grandma extends her hand, and I grab on to it like a lifeline. I then see the dead woman who's supposed to be my mother. I flash on the last time I saw her alive, in my bedroom. She looked tired. Worried. But that's what I think now. I wasn't thinking anything at the time. She was just my mother then, a sweet creature who lived for us. Now she's lying here with a puffy, chalk-white face. Her mouth is a small stripe, her chin receding into her neck. My real mother, the living one, is pretty. The green dress is buttoned up to the very top. Mom would never have wanted that. She looks almost Calvinist.

"Can I touch her?" My voice feels like it's coming from my stomach and sounds like Chonk's whining.

"Of course, sweetie."

I sit down beside her and take her hand. Its cold stiffness makes my eyes tear up. I'm trembling. Grandma hugs me, but I brush her off. Her arms won't help me. Luuk appears to have run off. "Great idea, Tineke, really excellent!" I hear Dad say, his voice breaking as he goes after Luuk.

Grandma's crying now too as she says, "Go on, it's alright. Give her a kiss."

And I do. Her once-soft cheek feels like rubber.

"None of us know how to do this, sweetie."

"You do," I say.

"Not at all. I didn't before, and I still don't. And this time is worse. Your grandpa was . . . I knew he was suffering a lot. I couldn't tell with your mom. I feel terrible about that."

I stroke Mom's cheek. Her body is already becoming less frightening.

"She didn't want this, Grandma. Someone else did this."

"Do you find that idea, that someone else is responsible, comforting?"

"Less. But it's how it is."

"The police did a full investigation."

"They didn't investigate everything."

"What didn't they investigate, Lies?"

I want to confide in her so badly, but it feels like I'd be breaking a pact with Mom if I did. I'll only hurt them more when they see the images. And after all that, they'll still say it doesn't prove she was murdered. God might just have been the person to push her over the edge. I want to get him myself. That's my promise to Mom right here, right now. He'll pay. He won't ever be able to do this to another woman.

"Lies? Like what?"

I shrug. "Never mind."

Dad and Luuk come back in. I give a saintly smile like Grandma does. "Come on, Luuk. It's not scary. Mom's asleep. She looks very sweet." That's what happens to you when you grow up. You get better at lying all the time.

He approaches, reluctantly. "Is it really Mom?" he asks.

"Yeah," I say.

He wraps his pale white arms around my waist. I feel him freeze up. My nose is in his neck. He smells of cookies and grass. I wait for his little shoulders to start shaking, but it doesn't happen. "You can touch her if you want."

He caresses her hand with his index finger. "She seems fake."

"Yeah."

"Like a doll. Like it's not Mom at all."

"Your mom's here," Grandma says. "Inside you."

Bullshit, I think, but I don't say it. My mom's lying in this coffin. She's no longer here. She's gone. She can't love us anymore or hold us. She can't hear us, see us, feel us. She's not within us, not looking down on us from some cloud, not waiting at some gate or other until we're dead too. Such stories might comfort other people, but not me. I miss her so much it feels like my heart was torn out of me, along with my stomach and intestines. The coffin is hideous.

Back on my phone in the car, I see I have a message on Tinder.

Good morning, beautiful. What a pleasant surprise that we're a match. I'm not really into chatting, let's meet up for a drink and see if the match holds up. Ohm, Nude.

24.

"Holy shit," Mees says. I rode to his house immediately, and I'm still catching my breath. We're in his room, which is really warm and messy. A mound of clothes, an unmade bed with a dirty white sports sock on it, a desk covered in Red Bull cans, pens, a half-empty bag of paprika chips.

"I didn't expect it to happen this quick. Do you think he's on to us? Maybe it's a trap. It's the exact same message he sent my mother."

"So now what?" He grabs the two-liter bottle from beside his bed and hands it to me. "Want some Coke?" Lukewarm Coke. Boys are a mystery.

"Him and his 'Nude,'" he sneers.

"Should I ask why he calls himself that?"

"Yeah."

I type: *Hey, Nude, what's with the nickname?*

"Lies, how would you go about a date like this? You're seventeen."

"We can arrange to meet at a hotel room."

"This isn't a soap opera."

"What do you suggest, then?"

"First of all, you don't know for sure that it's him yet. Secondly, if it is him, you don't know if he really killed your mother. Sorry, hate to say it . . . No doubt he did a number on her, but even then she might have, you know . . . done it herself."

He sits beside me on the bed. I'm in no mood for the suicide theory.

"It smells in here, you know that?"

"I don't smell anything."

Funny how boys don't smell themselves.

"Either way, this is extremely dangerous."

"Please don't tell me we should go to the police now."

"Has he answered yet?"

We look at my phone.

My psychologist once advised me to imagine myself "naked like a baby," hence Nude. And what about you, Fleur? What's a beautiful therapist like yourself doing on something so vulgar as Tinder?

"What an ass," Mees says.

I wanted to look around a little on here, but you're right. It is vulgar, I type back.

"Your mom's friend Kim," Mees says. "She knew about this date, didn't she? Maybe we should tell her what's going on."

"We don't have to really meet him, do we? We just need to find him. And follow him. Break into his house, steal his phone."

"Or hack him," Mees says.

I sigh and cover my eyes with my hands. We're just goofing around. Childishly. What was I thinking? That I'd go to the Okura bar all dolled up? We should take this information to the police. But then what? They'll have a little chat with God. And then? They'll let him go and tell me yet again that I need to accept that she killed herself.

What do I want? I want to butcher him like he butchered my mother. *Naked like a baby.* Have him crawl across the floor, bleeding, in tears and begging for mercy. I feel my anger like a pain in my body.

"Look, Lies, he's answering again."

I think we should meet up to exchange views on this. I'm looking forward to it already. Give me your number, then I'll message you a date and location.

"That easy, huh?" Mees says.

"You just mentioned hacking. Can you do that?"

"I think so. But if he's really the one responsible, he'll have taken precautions."

"He's a psychopath who thinks he's untouchable. He'll probably just keep going now."

"That's what I mean. I don't think it'll be that easy. You know what's easy? Hacking women. That's what he did, obviously."

I think of my mother's codes and how easy those were to crack.

"So before you give him your number, change all your codes and passwords. Don't use anything with the name of your dog, brother, or father, or your birthdate. Or your email address, your Apple ID . . ."

"Or we could just give him a different number and let him in. We'll give Fleur the usual accounts. Facebook, Insta . . . everything."

"In the end, an actual Fleur has to meet him . . ."

"In the end, once we've found him, we'll do that."

"And what then, Lies?"

"We'll make him confess."

"You wish."

"Don't be a jerk." I cozy up to his lanky frame, rest my head on his chest. I feel his tentative hand on my side. "She was really cold," I say. "I stroked her cheek. I promised her I'd get him." I rub my nose against his T-shirt, in the hollow under his chest. "She left her story behind. She didn't do that for no reason. She wrote it down so someone would find it, to let us know what kind of crazy person she was dealing with."

His fingers are inching toward the strap of my Calvin Klein bra. "I don't think she'd have wanted you to go after this guy by yourself."

"Do you think he knew about the document she wrote?" I ask.

"He wiped her computer remotely, but that's probably because of the photos."

I bring my mouth to Mees's face. I want to feel something. Something besides anger. I start with my tongue. Tentatively, his own meets mine. His hand on my bra strap is trembling now. I can feel his

The Grown-Up

warm breath on my cheek. Our mouths are wet and salty from eating chips. I put my hands beneath his sweater. His skin is soft like a baby's. We lie down on his bed. I don't know what to say anymore, and he doesn't seem to either. Mees throws the dirty sock in a corner. Then he caresses my face, and our eyes really meet at last. His cheeks are red and blotchy. He starts fumbling with my jeans, and I help him unbutton them. We're both afraid to look down. His fingers don't seem to have a clue where to go.

He pulls up my sweater, followed by my bra. I lie down on my side a bit because I barely have breasts when I'm on my back. Mees kisses and fondles them. I have to pee, but I'm afraid to get up now. We might be interrupted at any moment. By his mother, or because one of us has second thoughts, out of shame, common sense, or feelings of guilt. Is it weird to have sex while your mother's laid out in some cold morgue? Your mother, who maybe died because of this same desire? Will there ever be a day when I no longer think such things? And when is what we're doing even sex? When his penis is inside me? His finger?

I squeeze my eyes shut and try to focus my attention on the hand in my pants. I'm afraid to help him or he'll think I masturbate a lot. I shift myself on top of him. That's better. My breasts feel bigger this way, and I feel more in control. We take off our sweaters at the same time but lack the nerve to start with our pants just yet. I rub my pelvis against him, and I think I feel that he's gone hard. Or maybe he hasn't, but he seems to like it, because he eagerly meets my thrusts. We French-kiss more intensely now, our mouths open wider, tongues out. He holds my breasts. I'm on fire. My jeans are starting to chafe my crotch. He pinches me. I'm no longer the one doing the rubbing. I sit up straight, our mouths apart. His eyes are fixed on my breasts, which I press together with my arms. He purses his lips like he's about to blow smoke rings. I notice I'm not turned on anymore. I observe him as I rub against his crotch, the fire between my legs reminding me more of a bladder infection now than of orgasms. I think too much. I don't know if I'll ever be able to stop doing that, but I want to very much.

It stops as suddenly as it began. Mees pulls me toward him and holds me tight against his wet, heaving chest. A shiver runs through him. "Oh dear," he sighs. He smells of bleach. "I'm sorry," he whispers, but I don't know what for. Everything feels awkward all of a sudden for some reason.

"I need to go," I say. I hastily gather my clothes.

"But what are we doing now?" Mees asks.

"No idea. Nothing."

"I mean us. With each other."

I put on my T-shirt and sweater. If only I could sink into the ground.

"I'm a bit confused right now," I say and bolt through the door, down the stairs, without saying goodbye to his mother. All of a sudden, I can't stand the fact that he still has one of those.

25.

Kim lives two blocks down from Mom's place in a similar townhouse. She's a physical therapist who runs her practice out of her home.

She opens almost immediately after I ring the bell, her two cats writhing around her legs. Warm air that smells of soup emanates from inside.

"Hey, Lies! What a surprise, sweetie. Come on in." We hug, and I follow her into the living room, which is almost entirely taken up by a gigantic purple sofa, on which there's an open newspaper. "I just made ramen. Want some?"

I shake my head.

"Some tea, then? Or coffee?"

"Coffee would be great."

"Cappuccino? How about some cake with it? Or a cookie? I think I still have one left . . ."

Kim loves food. *Food's a medicine for everything,* she always says. She's been single for years. She'd have liked to have children, but she felt she had to do that within a relationship. Unfortunately, she never met the right potential father.

She puts my cappuccino down on the coffee table and plops down beside me, a bowl of ramen in hand. The smell makes me a bit nauseous.

"You went to see your mom, right?" She gives me a sad glance. "How was it?"

"Awful."

"I went too. It's hard to take in. So . . . unreal." She puts her food down and pushes it away. "I miss her so much."

"You knew, didn't you, about Mom and that man?"

Kim gets back up and walks over to the window. She stares outside for a long time. "Yes, I know she went out with him one night. And that she didn't hear from him after that. I advised her to let him go, and I think she did."

"Well, no."

"How do you know that?"

"I just found out." I don't feel like telling her about the file.

"I get why you refuse to believe your mother would—"

"This isn't about what I believe. It's about what I know."

"The police looked into everything. They retraced her every step. I talked to them for hours." She looks at me. "You didn't tell the police about the man."

I take a sip of my coffee. "Do you know what he called her?"

"No idea."

"You know."

"Alright, yes. Twigs. Well, that says it all, doesn't it?"

"What do you mean? What exactly does that say?"

"That he's insane. Like I said, after she told me about that date, I told her she should break things off with him immediately. I think she did. In any case, I never heard her talk about him after that. But I do think he pushed her over the edge. She became more distant after that date, a little weird. Bright and cheery one moment, gloomy and stressed the next. She lost weight, was tired all the time. Surely you noticed it too?"

I nod, but it isn't true. I can see it now, in hindsight, but I didn't before she died. My mother seemed the same as always. I wanted to be with her, and when I was with her I did my own thing, content that she was nearby. What teenager constantly pays attention to her mother? She could be a bit snippy at times, occasionally sad, but all that was to be expected since she still loved Dad. That was my take on it at the time.

"I'll be honest, Lies, since you're old enough, and you deserve the truth." Kim sits down opposite me on the coffee table. She grabs my hands. "I sometimes wonder if this Godfried really exists."

"Of course. So do I. He made up that name."

"No, honey. I mean I wonder if that date even happened."

I look into her eyes. I'm not sure what she's getting at. "You think Mom made it all up?"

"I wouldn't say 'made it up,' exactly. Your mother was quite vulnerable after the divorce. She just kept fretting and brooding. Slept poorly. She missed you and your brother an awful lot when you were with your dad. Maybe there was a date, maybe there wasn't, but the woman we both knew would have run from an idiot like that."

I rub my elbows. They're itchy. Everything's itchy all of a sudden. "So you're saying she lied about this? I don't understand."

"Perhaps she was just trying to make her life seem better, or worse, than it really was. Or maybe that wasn't it at all. All I'm saying is she was losing her mind a bit."

Now it's my turn to get up and walk toward the window. Even I'm beginning to doubt Mom's state of mind now. *She was just trying to make her life seem better or worse than it really was.* But I saw the photos, heard his voice. I read about how she shut out her only friend. "Why would she make up a thing like that?" I say, turning around again.

Kim picks at her fingernails, which are polished red and peeling. "Did your grandma tell you your mom had a wild imagination when she was a child? At school, she'd say her mother had been on the train that was hijacked by terrorists. Or she'd walk around with her arm in a sling for a week and claim someone tried to kidnap her in the park."

No, Grandma never told me about that.

"Your grandfather was already struggling at the time. Your mother likely fled into a make-believe world. Children who grow up in families where there's lots of lying, or where people regularly keep things from one another, start to tell lies themselves. For attention, or for the opposite: to deflect attention. Jet told me all this herself."

If this theory were true, just how much would Luuk and I have to be making up by now?

"That's what I thought of when she told me about him. She couldn't bear to be alone. She was ashamed of it, and it caused her great suffering. Sometimes she'd say she had a date, but then I'd ride by and see she was home that evening. She didn't show up at Pilates and would constantly have shady excuses. I once ran into her dressed all sexy at the supermarket. She wasn't herself. It worried me, to be honest. I talked with Peter about it."

"I'm sure she appreciated that."

"I didn't know what else to do."

"Talk to her, maybe?"

"I tried, but she flew into a rage, got insanely angry. She backed off even more after that. I told her she should seek help and work a bit less for a while."

My stomach is growling. Mom didn't make up stories. I'd have noticed if she did. I pinch the bridge of my nose.

"Do you really not want any ramen? Or maybe a sandwich? I bought some excellent cheese."

"No thanks."

I'm angry at Kim. None of this is her fault, but I'm mad anyway. Mom probably felt Kim didn't believe her. That's why she couldn't confide in her after things got out of hand.

"Didn't you ever consider the possibility that she was still seeing him? That she was acting weird because of that? That he was real after all?"

"Yes, I'm thinking that now that you say it."

"Do you have any idea how fucked up it is not to believe someone because a thousand years ago, as a child, they had a wild imagination?"

"She once told me she became a psychologist in order to better understand herself."

The Grown-Up

"So? What does that prove? Everyone keeps looking for reasons to believe her death was her fault. If you line up all your worst characteristics, you'd come across as a depressed, lonely madwoman too."

Kim chuckles and bites her lip. "Point taken."

Our house still looks like our old life might start again any moment. The decrepit trampoline in the front garden, the overgrown fence, Mom's bicycle chained beside the front door. I'd expected one of those police lines to be hanging here, but I'm able to go right in with my key. Inside it smells the same: part Mom's expensive scented candles, part fried rice, part Luuk's soccer cleats, which are under the coatrack, part Chonk. I don't know if I'm allowed to be here, but I think I am. The investigation was closed, our house is ours again. My phone rings. It's Dad. I mute the sound.

There's still some powder from the police investigation on the banister. How is it possible they found nothing relating to God? I go upstairs and try not to look at the photo of Mom, Luuk, and me hanging on the landing.

All the doors are open, and our beds have been stripped. When I enter my room, I feel like I'm dead and looking at my life like a ghost. The white curtains with big pink dots, which I chose with Mom at Ikea. My white desk full of paperwork and makeup, the colored miniature paper lanterns around my mirror, the red heart-shaped rug in front of my bed. This is where I most liked to spend my time, secure in the absolute certainty my mother was downstairs.

Her bedroom smells fresh as always. I lie down on her sheetless bed, my nose in her pillow, searching for some trace of her. She'd tickle my back here, or the palms of my hands; she'd rub my cold feet until they were warm. We'd drink tea and eat chocolate, watch *Gossip Girl* on Mom's new TV, a ridiculously expensive thing she'd bought all of a sudden. It feels like one of those dreams where you're suddenly back at your old home, your old school, and it turns out your life there never ended. No one missed you, and you have an exam the following day.

I open the drawer of the nightstand on Mom's side. A MacBook charger, a vibrator, and an assortment of pill bottles. There are no patient names on the bottles, but the labels say what the drugs are: temazepam, Dormicum, Ritalin, something called finasteride, and clozapine. I google the last one. *Clozapine is not only effective against psychoses but can also help decrease aggression/suicidality and dependence on alcohol, drugs, and cigarettes.* Then finasteride: *Inhibits the effects of testosterone on the prostate and on the hair follicles in the skin. For use in cases of urinary problems caused by an enlarged prostate. In case of baldness: after 3 to 6 months, you'll notice some hair growth on previously bald spots.*

These pills aren't Mom's. She might have taken a pill every now and then to sleep, but she wasn't balding. I also can't remember seeing all these bottles before, even though I'd looked in this drawer often. The last time was with Evi to show her my mother had a vibrator too.

These are God's pills, so he's been here.

I grab the bottle of finasteride and put it in my bag.

26.

Why am I going? I ask myself this constantly, questioning this desire of mine. There are two competing voices in my head. *You're throwing yourself to a wolf,* one says. *Let go and live for once,* says the other. The second voice won. I'm telling everyone I'm going to a convention. I hardly had to explain a thing. Kim took me at my word; the kids are with their father, and he's quite content to have them there. It feels like I'm being unfaithful. And I am. Unfaithful to myself, acting against my better judgment. Meeting up with a man who's sweet at times, then a bit of a bully, who disappears from the face of the earth one moment, then starts stalking me the next. Someone addicted to conflict, who treats me like a pet, and then the moment I surrender goes on the attack. I know better. But it's exciting, and I'm so consumed by that excitement there's no time to think about how my family's fallen apart. What does it matter if I go? I'm letting myself have this adventure. I just need to see his behavior for what it is: a game intended to subjugate me. Am I in love? Yes, I'm afraid so. I'm blindly heading for a brick wall without any brakes. Just let me do it. I'm going to London, I'm going to have all-consuming sex with a man who wants to eat me alive. I want to have that experience.

When I seat myself in the first row of the plane, a seat he reserved for me ("Only seat 1A is good enough for my Twigs"), I feel like a shameless mistress, like the woman who gets flown in, an expensive call girl.

He's not at the London airport. I don't know what I was expecting. God waving a balloon by the exit? Me running into his arms? Maybe. My mother says I have an overactive imagination.

I smile away my disappointment when I see a man in a suit holding a sign in front of him with my name on it. We shake hands, and I follow him to the black town car. What the fuck am I even doing here? I'm letting myself be summoned like a hooker. I'm lying to my children. What if something happens to one of them while I'm here? Or to me? I've promised them I'll always be there. That I'll always put them first. Not like their father, with all his cheating and moving on. And yet what am I doing? And all for a bit of sex?

All throughout the drive to London, I stare absently out the window. The rain makes the city as gray and oppressive as my guilty conscience. The chauffeur points out Big Ben to me, Tower Bridge, Buckingham Palace, Hyde Park, the Harrods shop windows. I say yes, no, and thank you at all the right times, but everything he says flies right past me. I might as well have been driving through a town in my own country.

"Well, here we are, miss," he says. He turns left and stops in front of an imposing set of stairs beneath a blue marquee. "Welcome to The Ritz." A man in a suit opens the door on my side.

"Welcome, Jet," he says, and I recognize his voice. He bows and takes off his top hat for me.

"Oh my God." I laugh and then put my hand over my mouth. He lifts me off my feet, and we shake with laughter, right there in front of the chauffeur and the porters. Suddenly everything is wonderful.

"Twigs!" he crows. "Come, hand me your suitcase."

In the room, he immediately throws me onto the red plaid velour blanket that covers the large bed. He takes off my shoes, my socks, tugs down my pants, and then presses his nose between my legs. He traces the waistband of my black lace panties with his finger. My body is ready for sex, but my mind isn't there yet. I haven't seen him for two months.

The Grown-Up

"Wait." I sit up again. He looks at me, his head still in my lap. I stroke his hair. The bald spot is gone.

"Hi," he says.

"Hi," I say.

"So here you are."

"Yeah."

"Lay down and turn over for me." He hasn't noticed that I'm feeling distant.

"Shouldn't we catch up a bit first?"

"We have the whole weekend for that."

"For this too."

"Come on, don't be a drag. Turn over. You're so beautiful. That ass. Those sexy panties. Please. I want to take a picture."

Who wants to be a drag? Not me. I do what he asks, and it turns me on. I sit on the bed on my hands and knees, my ass up high, still wearing my white shirt. "Not my face," I say.

"Don't worry. Only your amazing ass will show. So I'll have something to remember you by when you go back."

His fingers pull the crotch of my panties to the side. What we're doing is hot. It's also unwise. I cover my face with my hair. I feel his tongue against me. Is he still taking photos? His tongue is moving slowly, slowly . . . lingering, gently making circles. I've reached that place where I forget everything, where all I am is the place where he's licking me. He stops.

"Now that's what I call an appetizer. A foretaste of what's to come."

I pull the plaid blanket over me. As unashamed as I felt a moment before, I feel equally naked now.

"Oh, that thing," he says, looking at the blanket. "Do you have any idea how dirty it is? How many people have screwed on it? And how often do you think they send it to the laundry? Never, I suspect." He walks over to the bathroom.

I kick off the plaid blanket and crawl under the spotless white comforter. The room is nearly as tall and large as my entire house.

Heavy curtains hang in the windows, bound shut with a gold cord. There's a large fireplace opposite the king-size bed and a white gold drapery with embroidered crowns above me. The toilet flushes, the shower is turned on. The what-am-I-doing-here feeling takes hold again. To help me ignore it, I decide to unpack my suitcase. I put on one of the bathrobes, which is far too large, and pour myself a glass from the crystal bottles on the Biedermeier table, adding two ice cubes. I can't believe I'm here. That I'm doing this.

There's an empty shelf in the closet. His clothes are neatly ironed and folded, like he's been staying here for weeks already. The guy apparently lives in hotels. Or does he? I don't know a thing about him. He could be married, have children. I'm also unsure if I really want to know all that. Perhaps I'd rather stay in this strange bubble, where nothing is entirely self-evident.

Most of all, I want him to finish what he so lasciviously started. He spends a ridiculously long time in the shower. His phone and planner are on the nightstand beside the bed.

"Did you peek?" He's standing in the doorway, his hair wet, wearing the same oversized bathrobe I am.

"No," I say. I chuckle. "I wouldn't dare."

"Be honest."

"Of course I didn't. I put my clothes in the closet and poured myself a glass of whiskey. Want some?"

"You'd never admit to doing it."

"I'd never do it."

"Sure you would. Except you're too afraid."

I feel rather warm all of a sudden. "Do you want some whiskey?"

"I'll hold off on drinking for a bit."

A completely different God seems to have emerged from the shower.

"Should we get some sleep?" he asks, and then walks past me to the bed without saying another word.

He falls asleep with his arm and one leg draped over me. I can see the twilight outside through the gap between the curtains. I've never been to London. I want to hit the streets, see the city. When I try to turn over, he grips me even tighter. I scoot over a bit, and he rolls on top of me. He gently bites my neck. "Twigs," he says in a voice hoarse from sleeping. He reaches down, grabs himself, and begins to fuck me. Once he's come, he says: "You'll get your turn later, just wait."

There's a knock at the door. "Ah, there they are." He turns on the lights, slips into his bathrobe, and runs to the door. Two waiters follow him inside, one pushing a wheeled table full of silver platters. "Surprise! All for you, darling."

The tables are placed in front of the bed. One waiter uncorks the bottle of champagne, the other has God sign for the tab. When they've left, he dances around the table happy as a child. "Look at this, Twigs. It's a feast! All for you!"

I pretend to be happy and surprised.

"Come on, let's eat it in bed." He removes the silver covers from the plates, revealing two enormous cheeseburgers with French fries. I burst out laughing, genuinely now. He really is like a child. Like a little boy.

We eat and drink in bed. The cheeseburger is heavenly, as is the champagne.

God's still drinking only water.

He asks about my ex-husband and where things went wrong between us. I tell him Peter fell in love with someone else and decided to move in with her.

"Painful."

"Yeah."

"I'd go mad."

"I did in the beginning."

"Oh really? How?"

"I attacked him once. Scratched his neck with my fingernails. He'd just admitted what he'd been denying for months, namely that he was in love with her."

"Wonderful."

"What's wonderful about it?"

"That psychologists go mad once in a while too. And did you ever cheat on him while you were together?"

"No," I say. I don't know why I'm lying to him.

"Never? Not even a teensy-weensy bit just once? Slip of the tongue?"

"Well, maybe once in the pub when I was drunk. But things were technically over with Peter then."

"And how would you describe the difference between 'over' and 'technically over'?"

"He needed more space, felt we were going too fast, and wanted a weekend for himself. We were still students. This was long before our marriage."

"Aha. So 'technically over' actually means 'not over, just a bit of space.' And you immediately pounced on someone else."

I resist the urge to defend myself. "If that's how you want to put it, go ahead."

"Good to know."

"How are your studies coming along?" I'm in no mood to talk about myself anymore, much less about that period.

"They're on hold at the moment. Too busy doing business."

I lie down with my head in his lap, relieved at how our bodies are again becoming more comfortable with each other.

"Do you think I'm crazy?" he asks, after a long pause.

"I don't know you all that well yet."

"That's no answer."

"As a psychologist, I can't say someone's crazy."

"But as a human being. As a woman."

"As a woman, I find you . . . elusive." I'm afraid to use the word *unbalanced*.

"Why?"

"Because you can be really intense one moment, doing everything you can to win me over, then absent-minded and uninterested the next. I haven't heard from you in two months. I thought you'd forgotten all about me."

"I definitely wanted to forget you."

"Why?"

"Because I don't want to get attached. That only leads to trouble."

"Is that something you can even choose?"

"Absolutely. If a person starts to develop feelings for someone, they can dive in or run away."

"Unless their feelings are so strong they can't run anymore."

"I run before it reaches that point."

"Then why am I here now?"

"So I can test you."

"Test me how?"

"To see if you're a fling, or something more. Or less."

"And if I turn out to be more, you'll disappear."

"Probably. Same if you're less, to be honest."

"Do I have a say in it?"

"It's already obvious you're crazy about me."

"So you're saying I'm on temporary probation."

He laughs and tops off my glass. The two of us share a laugh at my expense. This isn't healthy, and I'll end up with my heart in a thousand pieces, but I stay. I lie back, revel in feeling my flesh against his, convince myself I can handle all this just fine—enjoying the moment, the scene's ugly ragged edges. I'll be home again in two days.

We kiss. He moans and fondles my breasts. We eat the salad and fruit, listen to each other's favorite songs on Spotify.

"Maybe none of this is real," he says.

"It's definitely not real," I say. "That's what's so wonderful about it."

"Maybe I don't even exist."

"You mean I've dreamed you up?"

"Yeah."

"You're rather complex for a figment of my imagination," I say with a chuckle.

"You're rather complex yourself."

"Am I your fantasy too?"

"Of course, sweet Twigs." He licks my cheek.

We make love, this time with an orgasm for me too. Afterward, I go to the bathroom. I choose not to read the labels of his pill collection again. I want to enjoy a fun weekend free from doubts or objections. When I return, the room is completely dark and he's snoring. I crawl up against his warm body and fall asleep.

It's still dark when I wake. For a moment, I don't know where I am. It feels like my children are a galaxy far away. I turn around. God's staring at his phone. I ask if anything's the matter.

"Why should there be?"

"You're checking your phone at night."

He puts it away and lies down with his head between my breasts. "I was bored."

I pet his dry hair.

"Jet lag," he mumbles. "Always tired. Always awake."

"That sounds awful."

"Should we go out?"

"Now?"

"Absolutely! I know an excellent club. Nearby. Let's get some fresh air."

"I don't know. Is this . . . ?"

"Come on, don't be a bore. Let's go."

It's dark and crowded at Tramp, which God says is where Rihanna recently celebrated her birthday. We're led to a table for two, and God is handed an illuminated wine list. I don't know where to look first. Young, beautiful people are everywhere, gleaming with confidence, as if born to dance here under these massive crystal chandeliers.

"This is all part of the arrangement, darling," God says. It's almost as if he's grown taller. His shoulders are straighter, his grin wider. Beside

The Grown-Up

him in his black suit, next to all these size-zero girls in sequined dresses under purple lighting, I feel like a country bumpkin.

"Oh no," God says when I confess this. "You need to stop thinking like that. You're a hot little dish. And smart! A total catch."

He kisses me. When he slips his tongue into my mouth, I can't help myself from looking over his shoulder to see if people are watching us.

"No one's paying attention. It's funny. We all think other people see all our flaws, but really everyone's just busy with themselves. It's possible to take things quite far without anyone caring. Watch."

He unbuttons his pants and takes out his penis. I instantly feel myself start to blush. "Put it back," I say. "Please." Over his shoulder, I see our waitress approaching with a bottle in a cooler.

"See? You're ashamed of me now, but to everyone else around us we don't even exist. No one saw me. No one heard you. We can flaunt ourselves however we like, but we're nobody to anyone else. That's why we can do as we please. We're free."

The waitress opens the bottle of white wine at our table.

"A little Montrachet for my girl." He practically has to scream over the pounding hip-hop beat.

I watch him: the way he flirts with the waitress, gets out his wallet, and gives her a big tip. Why does this man feel such a need to impress?

"I can't drink an entire bottle of wine myself," I say.

God chuckles. "They don't do glasses in a place like this, darling."

He takes a sip of his Perrier. He's apparently sticking to his habit of not drinking himself while getting me hammered.

We get up to dance, at first close against each other, then our bodies apart. I haven't done this in years, and why's that? Before meeting Peter, I liked nothing better, and I'd go from club to club every night.

"You're not a bad dancer for a Twigs," he says.

I put my hands in the air and remember I used to get by not on my looks alone but rather on how I moved my body. I twist my hips, shake my butt. I may be overdoing things a bit, but I want him to see I don't exist for him alone. Other men follow along, match my rhythm.

"See?" I say to him. "Other people see me too. I actually exist in real life." I throw my arms around his neck, but he brushes me off and turns away from me.

"What are you doing?" I ask.

"Going to take a piss."

I wait for him at our table. It's taking a long time. I have another glass of wine, and another. I'm embarrassed, sitting all by myself like this. Could something have happened in the bathroom? I walk over and wait in the hallway, leaning against the walnut panels. No sign of God. Someone offers me coke. I decline with a smile and head back to the dance floor. He's not there either. When I return to our table, the waitress is clearing the glasses.

"He just left," she says. "Don't worry, he paid."

It's drizzling outside. I check my phone. No messages. Did I do something wrong? I retrace all my steps from the moment we went into the club. What did I say? What did he say? Is this a game, a joke? Did I misunderstand something or miss it completely? Maybe he's ill, or there was something in his drink, or someone he'd rather not run into showed up. But then wouldn't he have waited for me or left a message? Sent me a text or called? I call him, but he doesn't answer. It's pouring now. The porter hands me an umbrella.

It's dark in the room when I get back. I'm reminded of the evenings I spent worrying when I was still with Peter. The confusion, fear, doubts. Stress hormones surging through my body. *It's all in your head, Jet. There's nothing the matter.* I know I've done nothing wrong and I still feel guilty. *How could you be this stupid? Think about what you're doing.*

"Sorry," I say. I can't help it.

I hear him turn over in bed. Obviously, I should pack my suitcase and leave. But I'm angry. "Would you mind telling me why you left all of a sudden?"

"Can I just sleep first?" he murmurs.

"No," I say. "You can't do this to me. I have to know what happened."

The Grown-Up

"Nothing, Twigs. Let it go."

I turn on the lights.

"Hey!"

"I came here for you. You decide everything in this . . ."

"In this what? Relationship? Is that what you want to say?"

"No. You're the one making the decisions, that's all. And that's fine. But you can't just abandon me like that. That's where I draw the line."

God sits up. He reaches for the glass on the nightstand and takes a sip. He then steps out of bed and stands in front of me, naked and smelling of sleep. "Can I trust you?" He points at me. "I wonder. You act so innocent. One of those wounded, lonely women. You seem grateful and happy for a second, but the next minute . . ."

"The next minute, what?"

"You're shaking your ass at the first guy you see."

"Is that it? That's why you walked off so angry?" I can't help but laugh.

"Go ahead and laugh. We're through as far as I'm concerned. I'm not in the mood for this. I'm getting a different room."

"Come on, this is ridiculous."

"That's what you think. How would you feel if I started hitting on other chicks right in front of you?"

"I wasn't hitting on anyone!"

"You were trying to make a point. That other men see you too." He starts to yell. "Fine, then! Go to them!"

My mouth goes dry. Who is this man? What could have happened to make him like this?

"I didn't mean to hurt you," I say softly. I pour myself a drink.

"You know, Sticks, you really drink too much."

"Fuck off." But he's right.

"Look, I was willing to give you everything in my power. In return, I expected to be able to trust you a hundred—no, a thousand—percent. I thought you were capable of that, but apparently not. I'm not saying you're bad, just not very trustworthy. That's not so strange; most people aren't. Most likely I'm not either. But I do need that in a relationship. A thousand percent, no more, no less."

Now he's the one talking about a relationship all of a sudden.

"Are you crazy about me, Jet?"

My legs feel like they're made of cement. I look at him, at his messy hair, his pale body, full lips, his angry eyes that seem almost pitch black now.

"It's better if I'm not," I say.

"Why?"

I don't know. I don't have an answer. I'm sure we'll burst out laughing any moment about all this. *Just kidding!*

"I don't know you," I say. "And you're doing all you can to keep it that way."

"But you like that, don't you? A little mystery, fantasy."

I shake my head.

"Do you want to know why I'm crazy about you? That little head of yours. What's inside it. Smart. But what am I to do with you? Seeing as you're so smart that you're manipulating me every which way. You shouldn't do that. Not to me. I don't take too well to that."

I've made him someone he's not, but he's done the same with me.

"Were you ever unfaithful to your husband, Jet? And don't lie this time."

"Twice," I say. "Once early in our marriage, with a good friend, during a weekend away. Once toward the end, with a colleague."

"Did you tell him?"

"No."

"Why not?"

"The first time was nothing, and I didn't want to hurt him. The second time was to get even. He was cheating on me, I knew it already. I felt terrible and rejected, and one evening I cried on a colleague's shoulder, which led to sex. The next day, Peter told me he was in love with someone else and he was leaving me. After that, I decided my fling with Jan wasn't technically cheating and so it wasn't any of Peter's business."

"Is this Jan still your colleague?"

"Yes."

"That's why you lied to me about this before."

"No. I just didn't feel it was any of your business."

"But it is. He's your other option."

"Oh no. Jan has a really nice girlfriend."

"So you were doubly unfaithful. Technically."

"It was a slipup and one time only."

"This is no time to start lying to me again."

How did I get into this ridiculous conversation?

"It's none of your business, Godfried. You and I didn't even know each other then. You act as if I've been unfaithful to you."

"You have. By lying."

"Not saying certain things isn't the same as lying."

"Love begins with full transparency."

"I disagree."

"Then what do you think love begins with?"

"With wanting to be sweet, and wanting what's best for each other."

God chuckles. "Alright, alright. Was what you did sweet?"

I notice he's getting hard. He's enjoying this. *If you've had it with the game, stop playing,* I always tell my clients. *And if you can't stop, ask yourself why that is. Maybe you're secretly enjoying it. Maybe it's familiar territory to you, these power struggles.*

But I'm on the ropes.

"See? You can't answer that."

"I think we should stop doing this. It's half past five. Let's get some sleep." I walk over to my side of the bed and take off my clothes with my back to him. I keep on my bra and panties.

"Do you still want me to get another room?"

"That's what *you* wanted."

"Because you're angry."

"Whatever. I'm going to sleep."

He crawls up next to me, and after I switch off the light, starts stroking my back with his finger.

"Twigs," he whispers.

I keep silent, pinching my eyes shut. He slowly inches nearer. *I have a very big problem*, I think. He kisses my neck, my shoulders. Pets my stomach. Do I want sex? I don't know. My body does, my mind doesn't.

We have slow sex. I'm so tired I'm crying.

"I told you we can be sweet to each other, didn't I?" he whispers. "That other stuff is just because I'm so crazy about you."

"And because you're afraid," I say.

"Utterly panicked."

The next morning, we follow the crowd through the city, holding hands. I look at shop windows, the red double-decker buses, the sprawling traffic, but I don't see a thing. The hand holding mine is like a handcuff. I don't recognize this feeling. I want him completely, and at the same time I want to run away as fast as I can.

"How many men have you been with?" he asks over coffee. He never, ever stops. We're sitting outside because I wanted to smoke. I quit two years ago, but now, in my confused state, smoking gives me some reassurance. Something of myself.

"I have no idea," I answer.

"Sure you do. Everyone does. Unless you've lost count already."

He's looking for pushback. The intimacy we finally shared last night has to be broken.

He closes his eyes. "There's three at least. Your husband, your colleague, and that really good friend of yours. What's his name?"

"I'm not doing this with you, Godfried."

"Why not? Normal lovers tell each other such things."

"We're not normal lovers. We hardly know each other. And you keep asking me for total openness, but how about starting with yourself?"

I'm shaking. From the cold, fatigue, these games.

The Grown-Up

"I'll be honest: I've lost count. But definitely over a hundred. That's what happens when you travel a lot."

"Why do you travel so much?"

"I'm in commerce. I buy things in China and Japan, and I sell them in other countries through an online shop. Websy. Just junk, really. My jade rollers are doing great."

I don't remember him telling me about this before.

"Google it."

"I believe you."

"Hey, Twigs. Still fretting, are we?"

I nod.

"You think I'm a weirdo."

"Yeah."

"I am. But I'm also crazy about you. And everything about you. That's not nothing, right?"

"No."

"Check your phone."

He's sent me a WhatsApp message with a video. I open it and see myself, which is to say, my ass, under horrible lighting, my face red and smooshed against a pillow, my vagina, his fingers, his penis. I quickly close it.

"Nice, isn't it? For later, when I'm gone. A souvenir."

27.

It's a beautiful, clear, but cold day. I lay awake all night next to Luuk, who couldn't sleep either. "Now Mom's dead, we're all a bit dead," he said at one point, and he's right. Once he started dating Laura, the father we knew disappeared too. We're orphans now. "We have each other," I told Luuk. All throughout the night, I felt a solemn responsibility to keep on living and take care of him. I can't let anything happen to me, so it's ridiculous to try to plan a date with God. I need to involve a grown-up in this, to tell Jochem everything I know.

"I'm so nervous," Luuk says, pushing his dry hair, which smells of straw, in my nose.

I hold him. I think Mom would prefer I be his new mother over Laura. "It's going to be alright, Luuk. You just need to keep thinking: *I'll get through this.* That's what I do."

The dress Mom gave me is hanging in my closet. Dark purple velvet with gold butterflies and a lace stand-up collar. Extremely kitsch. I think she bought it in London. I never wanted to wear it because I felt silly in it, but I'll wear it this afternoon, at her funeral.

Downstairs, Chonk jumps up against me, squealing with enthusiasm. If only I was a dog, unreasonably happy all the time. Laura's in the kitchen holding a large mug in both hands. She looks like she cried all night. I think of how odd it is for everything just to keep going when the worst thing that could happen happened. This afternoon, we're putting Mom's body in the ground. Meanwhile Laura's arguing

The Grown-Up

with Dad as usual, I'm making breakfast, and Luuk's playing video games. Like any of these things matter.

"Hey, sweetie," Laura says. "Sleep well?" She sounds like she has a cold.

"Not really."

"Luuk was with you, I assume?"

"Yeah."

I get two bowls, put them on the kitchen island, and fill them with milk.

"Want some tea too?"

"Alright."

Laura holds a mug under the water boiler. "With ginger?" Her chin trembles.

"What's wrong?" I ask.

In my eyes, everyone over twenty-five is old, but she looks like a child now, with her pale, makeup-less face and boring hair in a scrunchie.

"I can't get through to your father anymore," she says.

"Who can?"

"He's broken." She holds on to the bluestone countertop like she might fall over any moment. "He treats me as if I killed your mother."

"Maybe you did." I can't help myself. I want to hurt her. I want her to realize what she's done every day. A whole family broken up, all because she just had to have him.

"Oh God," she says, shrinking away. I see her press her fingernails into the ball of her thumb. "I'm sorry," she says. "Do you know how terrible I feel about everything? For all of you? How difficult this is for me? I don't know what to do. Leave? Is that what you want? What he wants?"

Honestly? Yes, that's what I want. Someone has to bleed.

"What did you expect?" I ask. "Some kind of happy, readymade modern family you could just step into? Did you think you could just build a new family on the ruins of the old one?"

Mom's alive. In me. Her voice. Everything she always wanted to say to Laura.

"No. I didn't expect that," she says. "Your father's the one who did. He wanted me, and he made quite a fucking effort to get me. He was married, I wasn't. He lied, I didn't. He left your mother, I didn't. But who gets all the blame, all the hate? Who gets ostracized at the office? Who needs to prove herself every day, on every birthday, holiday, any fucking day, again and again? Me. And why? Because I fell in love with him. Who has to figure out how to win your love? Not him."

"He's my father. I've known him all my life. I knew him when he was still in love with Mom. And whatever he says, he did love her. Now that she's been murdered, he suddenly remembers again just how much."

"Murdered?"

"Yes."

"That's really what you think?"

"Yes."

Dad enters the kitchen in his sweatpants. He doesn't appear to have slept either. His hair is standing up straight, and his beard, usually neatly trimmed, has grown out like a gnome's.

"Oh," he says, seeing the two of us there. You could cut the tension between Laura and him with a knife. He briskly pats my back in passing, then makes himself a double espresso. "Sweet Lies . . ." Then: "I'm going out to walk Chonk. See you in a little while, ladies."

When the door closes behind him, Laura starts to cry again. "I'm trying so hard," she says, sobbing.

"Maybe stop doing that," I say. "People who try hard are annoying."

I take the tea she made me and put the bowls of milk on the serving tray, together with the box of cereal.

"I spoke to your mother, not so long ago," she says suddenly. "Two weeks before she disappeared, I think."

I turn around.

The Grown-Up

"Something was up with Luuk at school. His teacher was worried about him and how withdrawn he is. He'd done rather poorly on his final test, despite being perfectly capable. Anyway, you know your parents don't talk to each other . . . The teacher had told your father about it, but she refused to discuss it separately with your mother. She felt they had to work out how to communicate with each other. One of the reasons Luuk's the way he is, she said, is this constant arguing between his parents. And I felt she was right about that. But your father refused to go see your mother. So I did."

"And she let you in?"

"Yes, which surprised me. She was quite friendly. In fact, she seemed happy to have someone drop by. To be honest, she was acting rather weird. Nervous and agitated. Frightened, even. The curtains were drawn in the middle of the day."

"Did you tell this to the police? Or Dad?"

"Yes, of course. 'She's losing her mind,' your father said. We got into an argument about it because I felt he had to help her. I'd gotten the strong sense she was afraid of something or someone. I asked her how she was doing, and she said she felt great. She had a boyfriend, but she wanted to keep you two out of it. She literally said, 'I'm not the type to play house with my new partner.' Your father didn't believe it. He said she had tended to exaggerate and often made things up. But ever since, I've wondered: Aren't we missing something here? I also got the feeling there was someone else in the house when I was there. Perhaps her boyfriend. In any case, it was clear to me this man wasn't exactly making her happy. I told the police this too, by the way. They didn't find anything there—no hairs, no fingerprints. But when I hear you say she was murdered, I don't think the idea's nonsense. Or she might have been driven to kill herself, or forced to. Someone was there. I can't prove it, and Peter refused to believe me, but I'm convinced there was."

"Is that what you two are always arguing about?"

"Our arguments are always about the same thing: your mother. He's like a broken record, always playing the same tune. Even now that she's gone."

"Especially now," I say. "They never got to say goodbye properly. They weren't through with each other yet. Not really."

We're silent for a moment. I try to think about my living mom and not the dead one. Laura makes fresh tea. It's an odd sensation to have the person I hated most up until now be the only one who believes me. But I don't trust her. This might just be part of a new offensive to win me over. I can hear Mom's furious laugh. *That girl. Come on, don't let her manipulate you.*

It's as if Laura can read my mind. "Look, I understand that you don't trust me, that you don't trust anyone. Your parents made a huge mess of things, and I was forced on you. Plus I know I'm too eager. When I first fell for your father, I thought I had love enough to get us through anything, love enough for his children too. But now . . ." She sighs. "Your father says your mother made things up. I think I'm guilty of the same. I made him up, our relationship and what drove it. In my mind, I turned him into a strong, sweet, romantic hero, someone who was brave enough to choose love over everything else. Absolute nonsense. He just used me as his safety net because he couldn't be alone."

"I guess it all worked out then," I say flatly. "By the way, you do know that you have to make it work now? Five hearts were broken as a result of that fucking divorce, Laura. Don't let it all be for nothing."

28.

I sleep fifteen hours when I get home. I don't know what to do with myself when I wake up. *You need to end this,* my mind screams. *Be clear.* I try to see myself the way I'd view a client.

You're vulnerable, and he took advantage of that. He's a master at identifying your unhealed wounds and finding your buttons, and he's attached himself to you by pushing them. Protect yourself. He can't be saved, he'll never change. I shower and get dressed. Then I pick up Chonk from Kim's, where I make up some excuse about why I can't stay for coffee. I walk back home, letting Chonk sniff every tree, every lamppost, every blade of grass along the way. I'm not talking to myself now but to God. I talk to him in my head all day, repeating the same thing like a broken record: *I can't see you anymore. I know now that we're a bad match. What we have is toxic, and it'll only end in misery.* That's why I need to break things off now, not at my house or in some hotel room. It needs to be a public place. These feelings of complete isolation, of failure, this urge to run away . . . I don't want this anymore. Love should be fun and cheerful, without games and tests. But what am I talking about? This isn't love. This is an illness.

When I get home, there's a vase in front of my door with a large bouquet of flowers. I don't need to see the card to know who it's from. I know how this man operates: love bombing. It's just one of the tactics narcissists use to get people to admire them. There's also a card on the doormat.

Sweet and uncommonly beautiful Twigs,

It had everything, that weekend of ours in London. Looking back, I can see it wasn't very nice of me to leave you hanging at the club. I'm just a jealous asshole. But take it as a compliment too: I wasn't like this with other women. Some of them even complained about it, about how I didn't seem to care if they flirted with anyone else. And I really didn't. Not until you came into my life with your smart and pretty little head. Let me make it up to you. I'll be back in the Netherlands this coming week. We'll have dinner, and you can pick the place.

Your God

His card makes me doubt myself again. Am I making him seem better, or worse, in my mind than he really is? Shouldn't I meet him one more time to know for sure?

After the flowers, he sends me "It Ain't Over 'Til It's Over" by Lenny Kravitz on WhatsApp and writes me sweet messages. I ask myself: *What do I have to lose by going? Is my life alone here, with my sofa and the TV, all that great?* I make up a thousand excuses, for going, for not going, but my better judgment has already lost out to my heart. I convince myself it's actually good for me to see him again, so I can be certain that what we have needs to end.

We've agreed to meet at a French bistro within cycling distance. When I walk inside, I see him at a small table illuminated by candlelight. It's warm inside. I have a stiff back, and my head is a mess. My once-rock-solid resolve to end things is starting to crumble already. After I dropped the kids at Peter's yesterday afternoon, a well of self-pity was waiting for me. Why should I deny myself this, when Peter has it all? What if I try not to take this so seriously? I've already forgotten how worthless I felt sitting outside that restaurant in London. My fear has given way to nervous desire. I see this meetup as a second chance. Maybe a whole weekend in London was a bit much for two damaged individuals who hardly know each other. Bistro Le Escargot is a somewhat less imposing environment.

He looks at me like he wants to eat me. His teeth are shiny white. He looks ridiculously handsome to me in his black turtleneck sweater. He stands and spreads his arms.

"There she is!" he cries, a bit too loud. Other guests look up from their meals. We embrace, and I notice myself tense in his arms.

He grabs my hand right away. "Did you miss me?"

I chuckle awkwardly.

"Well, I missed you." He pours me a glass of white wine. "Listen, Twigs. Before you say anything, I'm a weird one, I know. I wasn't nice to you in London. And now I'm quite afraid you've had me come here so you can dump me. There, I said it. If that's what you were planning, then do it now. Right away. And then I'll be on my way again. No hard feelings. But let me just say one more thing first: what you and I have, it's . . . electric. Magic. Like we have no choice. Free will has little to do with it. It's as if our souls click on a different level from our egos. Personally, I'd find it a pity if we let ourselves be led by a fear of commitment, but maybe you have different thoughts on that."

"Can I have a sip of wine first?" I ask, and he bursts out laughing.

As I settle myself at the table, he asks again. "Well, what do you think?"

"I have been thinking a lot these past two weeks," I admit.

"Tell me."

The waiter puts a basket of bread with garlic butter on the table. I take a piece, spread a generous amount of butter on it, and hand it to God.

"So. Is it over?"

I look into his eyes, and I can't do it. How do you break up with someone you're madly in love with? And isn't infatuation simply a form of psychosis, with the same fearful, crippling sensations? All the questions that have kept me awake at night these last weeks come flooding back. I flee into my role as therapist.

"Maybe we shouldn't stick a label on it," I say. "We like each other, so let's keep it fun and not make it so heavy right away. Remember, you didn't want to call what we have a relationship. Well, let's not, then."

"How would you describe what we're doing?"

"We're two people who get together to do something fun every now and then, like now. Going out to eat or the movies, giving each other time and attention, and slowly building on that. How do celebrities always put it?"

"'We're exploring our feelings for each other.'"

"Right."

"I don't like that. I like a thousand percent. Or nothing."

"Well, then this is an opportunity for you to challenge yourself. Who knows? Maybe you'll discover you're perfectly capable. Is it really necessary for things to be so heavy and dramatic all the time?"

He raises his glass, and I clink mine against it.

"To our q-ling," he says.

"Our what?"

"Quality fling. Or prela. Whatever you want to call it."

"Prela . . ."

"Prerelationship. Hey, it was in my profile: I play Tinder on level nine. Been there, done that, baby."

We eat and talk, calmly this time, and not about psychology or free will, but about ordinary things. His work, my work, my kids. He says he definitely wants children. I say I definitely want no more children. And even if I would, I can't anymore. "Why not?" he asks, and I answer that I'm too old, that my eggs have probably withered already. He claims anything is possible these days. Women in their fifties are having children. But, I say, should they want to? Is that best for the kids? A mom who's seventy when they're just embarking on adult life?

"It's actually quite good for kids if their mother or father dies when they're still young," he says. "My parents have been dead for quite some time already, and I haven't suffered a second because of it."

The Grown-Up

I smile. God and his life philosophies.

"Did you love them?"

"Honestly, no. At least I don't think so. My father never said anything. He was like a piece of furniture. My mother was depressed. She was in bed all the time. That's what I remember."

I picture him in our bed in London, curled up and in the dark.

"Do you have any brothers or sisters?"

"Thankfully, no. I have no obligations whatsoever. No family, no kids, no home. And no girlfriend, it turns out."

"But a q-ling."

"Right. A real catch."

I leave my bicycle and, no longer worried, get in the taxi with him.

"I have a surprise," he says.

"Are you coming to my place?"

"No."

"But Chonk is alone."

"We'll pick him up on the way."

"I need to go to Pilates tomorrow."

"So cancel it. Live a little."

After a long, bumpy road, we stop at a gate.

"We'll get out here," God says to the taxi driver, and he hands him a fifty. "This is great."

It's so dark here we need to use the flashlights on our phones.

"Where are we?" I ask.

"You'll see."

We begin to walk. Chonk follows with some hesitation, sticking close the whole time. Once my eyes adjust to the dark, I see we're in a vacation home community. God takes my hand and coaxes me along countless cottages, past a hideous building beside a sign that reads "RECEPTION" and some gardens with an arbor. We're silent. I'd promised myself I'd sleep at home tonight, not let him drag me along again. But here I am, following him through the night. I have no idea where I am, no idea where we're going.

"How much farther?" I ask.

"We're almost there," he says. "Try to relax. It's not like I'm going to kill you."

We pause where the path ends.

"Voilà," God says. He shines his flashlight at the umpteenth cottage. "That's it." He rummages in his pocket and pulls out a key. "Our palace." He giggles like a toddler and opens the front door. "Welcome, beautiful!"

He leaves his shoes outside. I step out of my own and walk inside in my socks. The floors are linoleum and curl up a bit in the corners.

"Is this place yours?" I ask.

"As of this afternoon. No more hotels. A place of my own. A place for us."

I follow him through the narrow hallway into the living room, which is filled with balloons. He was apparently confident I'd come with him. There's a small suitcase in the corner of the room next to an electric heater. It's sweltering in here. God opens the curtains and turns on the outside lights. "Look," he says, but I don't know what I'm supposed to see besides trees and bushes. "No busybodies, just green all around. I was told deer pass through here sometimes too."

He takes me in his arms and starts to kiss me passionately. "What do you think?" he asks between kisses.

I gently push him back. "It's great!" I lie. I see Chonk sitting in the doorway behind him.

"Naturally, we still need to furnish it, make it cozy. Break it in." His hands creep under my dress. My body's turned on. My head wants me to leave. "Why don't you sit on the sofa, and I'll get us drinks."

He goes to the kitchen and gets two glasses from the Formica cupboards, then opens the refrigerator and takes out a bottle—all while humming a tune. I've never seen him this cheerful. Chonk tentatively shuffles toward the sofa and jumps on it. I pretend not to notice. God takes off the wire cage and turns around suddenly, aiming the bottle in front of him as the cork pops and champagne gushes out. He runs

The Grown-Up

toward me, shaking the bottle, thoroughly drenching me. I'm so startled I scream and hit him right in the face. Chonk bolts to the front door, barking.

"What the hell?" I cry. I'm panting, my hand on my chest.

"Have you lost your mind?" I see his face go dark. "You hit me! Hit. Me!"

The champagne drips from my face and stings my eyes. Through the blur, I vaguely see his hand rise. I wince and realize I'm nowhere near civilization. No one will hear or see me. I prepare to dive for his legs as his hand descends. Suddenly it's on the back of my neck, and his forceful hand is pulling my face toward his, toward those soft lips, his tongue, dripping with champagne. I hear his deep laugh. He holds me tight and licks my face, howling with laughter. "That face! You should have seen that face of yours! What a sight! You were really scared, weren't you? You were thinking: *Holy shit, this guy's going to hit me!*"

I free myself from his grip and say there's nothing funny about it.

"Oh come on, Twigs. Can't you be a little spontaneous?" He takes a sip and passes me the bottle.

"You wasted it too," I say.

"Twigs, there's a thousand more bottles where that came from."

We lie naked on the light-brown leather sofa, which smells like the inside of rain boots. It's damp from the champagne and our sweaty bodies. The sex we just had felt more like we were fighting than making love. It wasn't like this with Peter, nor with any other man I've slept with. As if we wanted to destroy each other. It's frightening what happens when our bodies meet. I want him deeper inside me, ever deeper, want him to hurt me. I do it myself, put his hand to my throat. I want to be dizzy from lack of breath. When he forces me to my knees, pulls my hair, that's when I feel truly alive. I open my mouth and relax. Surrender. A body seeking pleasure. Nothing more.

When I hear him softly snoring a little while later, I crawl off him and get a blanket from the bedroom. I hold in my sneeze. Everything here is damp and dusty. God lies curled up like a fetus. I put the blanket over him and creep into the hallway with my clothes in my hands. I have marks from his hands on my thighs and his teeth on my shoulder. My vagina burns. Was I raped? No. I wanted it. I wanted it rough. But I have no idea what I want now. To be away from here, I know that much.

Chonk is still lying in front of the door. I put him on the leash and step outside, where it's getting light. I can hear birds and the motorway in the distance as I walk around the quiet cottage community. The other early birds out walking their dogs look at me like I'm mad. Homeless. A mess. I feel just as ashamed and guilty as I did after that one time with Jan. And just as sincere about what I think next: *I won't ever let this happen again.* But even as I think this, I know I'm lying.

It feels like I've been walking for hours already when I get back to the restaurant. As I unlock my bicycle, it begins to rain softly, but I hardly notice. All I can think of is God, my thoughts running in a loop. I remember how well the evening began. He has it in him. He was doing his best. He was cheerful, interested, even sweet. Is it possible he'd mellow out once we got to know each other better? Is it possible that he could change? *Come on, Jet, you're a psychologist. You know no one changes that much. Stop excusing everything. Put an end to it.*

The next Monday, I talk with my colleague Jan in the kitchen of my practice. It's after five o'clock. In the past twenty-four hours, God has sent seventeen messages, including a video in which he masturbates to photos of us in our room at The Ritz.

I tell Jan about a client of mine who's in a highly toxic relationship.

"That reminds me of a client I had years ago." Jan is seated on the kitchen counter with his alcohol-free beer. "She'd been stalked by her ex for years. By that point, he'd been issued a restraining order, but he kept coming to her house anyway. Finally, she made a deal with the police: they'd drive by every hour throughout the weekend and keep an eye out so they could catch and arrest him. Which ended up happening. But it turned out she'd been leaving the back door unlocked the whole time.

The Grown-Up

For him. They even had sex sometimes. He'd hit her occasionally, or they'd fight, and then she'd call the police. She was hooked on this cycle. She needed the police to put an end to it. At the time, I recommended she visit a clinic to work on her love addiction."

"Love addiction? Isn't it some extreme form of self-loathing? Some kind of self-harm? I think my client is unconsciously punishing herself..."

"It seems more like an excessive need for affection to me, combined with a strong sense of abandonment. Basically, it's pathological separation anxiety. The person will accept anything to not end up alone. The addiction is to the man's attempts to make it up to her. Those little sparks of love have the same effect as crystal meth. She craves more and more of the stuff all the time, but for that she has to suffer great pain first."

"But what I don't understand, and what annoys me about my client, is the duplicity. She comes to me to free herself from this man. She wants to get rid of him, but then welcomes him back the following moment."

Jan gives me a questioning look. "This annoys you?"

"Yes."

"Why this personal involvement? It's not good, Jet, to get annoyed with clients."

"I'm only human. She tells me the same story every week."

"Don't they all? You have a degree in this, darling. You know as well as I do why she does it."

"She doesn't see a way out anymore."

"She feels that she doesn't deserve better. And believes anything's better than to be alone. Remember how awful it was to quit smoking?"

I don't tell him I've secretly started again.

"It starts with a resolution. You feel it's a dirty habit, you despise yourself, you know it'll kill you, and this fear makes you crave another cigarette. You promise yourself you'll quit tomorrow. Or next month. You keep putting it off, and the addiction deepens. Smoking becomes a form of punishment. You do it because it once made you feel brave, rebellious, cheery. And you want to feel that again. Same thing goes for toxic relationships."

"Could she be hooked on the pain too?"

"It's possible. Or on being submissive? Many people feel ashamed of that."

"I don't think that's it. It's something in that feverish state. Almost like possession. Like he's taking control of her."

"Some people find strength in pain. Knowing they can survive something, that they won't break down. Suffering for love. Is your client someone who feels she has to earn love, that she doesn't deserve it unless she's worked for it?"

I get a beer from the refrigerator. Jan gives my back a friendly pat. It was in this kitchen that we had sweet, stupid sex almost two years ago. We were drunk, I was sad, and Jan comforted me. He came into my practice the following morning to ask if I wanted to talk about it. I told him I didn't, so we never did. It's fine like this. Our friendship and professional relationship never suffered as a result.

"How do these men do it, get someone under their thumb like this?" I ask.

"Women do it too. Don't underestimate them," Jan says. "Both parties manipulate by referring to each other's childhood pain, each other's childhood traumas. They recognize it in each other, often unconsciously. But you know all this yourself. I'm just mansplaining now. Why'd you bring it up?"

"Just to get some feedback."

"You're sure you're not too personally involved?"

"I have my own childhood pain."

"I know." Jan smiles. His bald head is shiny in the fluorescent lighting. If only God had Jan's character, his peace, his calm intellect. "This sounds to me like what you called it: a toxic relationship between a woman with tremendous separation anxiety and a man with narcissistic characteristics. Quite a dangerous combination."

"Right, I'd figured that much. But now what?"

The Grown-Up

"Now nothing. He'll leave her, or she'll leave him. Only then will she be able to move forward."

"But the situation's dangerous, you just said."

"There's nothing you can do about that. When two adults play with fire, all you can do is stand by and watch. You can tell her she needs to get out a thousand times, but she won't. Until she does."

I take a big gulp from my can.

"Not to pry or anything, but this wouldn't actually be you we're talking about, would it?"

"Oh no!" I laugh. I know he believes me. We've never lied to each other.

"Just be careful not to get personally caught up in it. You can always refer her to me."

I tap my can to his, then down the last gulp of lukewarm beer. My phone rings in my purse. There was a time I desperately wanted to hear that sound, the special ringtone I assigned to God. It nearly gives me a heart attack now.

When I'm in my car, I check my phone. He's called three times and sent two texts.

> Why aren't you answering?

> Quite a handsome fellow, that colleague of yours. I certainly hope he doesn't end up in your bed.

I start the engine and drive to Peter's place. I normally wait outside for Lies and Luuk to come out with their backpacks. I promised myself I'd never set foot in that apartment where he plays house with that bimbo. But I'm afraid to sit out in the street by myself now.

That night, Lies and I lie in bed wearing our flannel pajamas, a tray with two big cups of tea and a Toblerone bar between us. We're watching *The Voice*. I'm trying to enjoy myself. My phone's off. Lies presses her cold feet against my legs. As we stare at the TV and watch one of the judges put a female candidate through the wringer, Lies suddenly asks: "How do you know if you're in love?"

Her question brings me back to earth, out of my thoughts.

"Oh, sweetie," I say, and I stroke her cheek. "With who?"

"Mom, that doesn't matter. Just tell me."

"Well, you'd know if you think of this person constantly. And if you get butterflies in your stomach when you see him."

"Or her," Lies says.

"Is it a girl?"

"No."

"When you're in love, you can't eat and can't sleep anymore, and all you want is to be with this person all the time."

"Well, I'm eating and sleeping fine. But I do think about him a lot. Sometimes I think he's really stupid. And I'm afraid he thinks I'm really stupid. But we did kiss a little while back. At Evi's party."

I push the tray aside and pull her to me. She rests her warm head on my chest, and I stroke her hair. My throat is starting to swell. I've been so preoccupied with God that I didn't notice a thing. My sweet daughter, who's growing up right in front of me. The one I miss so dearly when she's with her father. Who always acts so tough but now is opening up all of a sudden. She wraps her arms around me.

"Why can't I always live here, Mom? Why should Luuk and I pay the price for your divorce? There's always something wrong. I had a bladder infection this week. How am I supposed to get help with that from Laura? Or from Dad? It was the same after that kiss: all I wanted was to be home with you."

"It's what we agreed, sweetie."

"I never agreed."

"Dad's doing his best, isn't he?"

"Not even close. And don't act all supportive of him now. I know you hate him."

"I don't hate him."

"I'm allowed to choose, by the way. I'm seventeen."

I feel like crying over everything that's gone wrong. We're all sweet, good, smart people, and we still screwed everything up beyond repair. Now Lies is in love, but instead of it being wonderful she sees it as something to be terrified of. It's Peter's and my fault.

"And don't ask: *Did you talk to Dad about this?*" She mimics my voice, high and silly. "Why should I talk to Dad about it? Why should I have to be the one to talk about the difficult things? Aren't my parents supposed to do that?"

Just imagine me bringing God into this mess. It's unthinkable. And I really have no desire to do that, no matter how awful I feel when I'm alone. I need to end it.

I need to be here for my children.

Those were the last words Mom wrote.

29.

Luuk comes into my room wearing the suit he bought with Dad. My heart breaks, but it breaks all the time now anyway.

"You look really sharp, Luuk," I say.

He looks at himself in the tall mirror on my closet door. "You think?"

"Mom would have liked seeing you looking like this."

"Really?"

I put on the velvet dress with the gold butterflies.

"It's weird, but I'm getting a bit used to it," Luuk says. His lips are chapped. I rub some eight-hour lip balm I stole from Mom on them.

"Getting used to what?"

"That Mom . . . that she isn't here anymore."

"You'll never get used to it, Luuk. It might seem like it for a little while, like now. But just wait, you'll feel it again tonight."

"What?"

"The loss. The feeling like your legs were cut off."

"I'm mad at her."

"Yeah."

"My teacher told me Mom was in so much pain she forgot she had to keep on living for us. I wonder: What kind of pain, exactly?"

"Your teacher needs to shut up. Mom did want to keep on living for us. You can't listen to idiots like that, Luuk."

"She was definitely in pain. When she died. Doesn't dying hurt?"

The Grown-Up

I hold him close. I'm his mother now. "Yes. But she doesn't hurt anymore."

Three big black limousines pull up in front. Mom's coffin is in the one in front. All kinds of people in the street are looking at us. It's starting to rain, and the men in black, as Luuk calls the attendants, lead us to the car while holding umbrellas over our heads.

The grown-ups are all wearing sunglasses, which I find silly. They argue.

"You're going in a car with your children, Peter," Grandma snaps. "Without Laura."

Laura looks like she weighs no more than thirty pounds in that simple black dress of hers.

"She'll ride with her own parents," Grandma goes on. "Why are these people here, anyway? Are they part of our family?"

Grandma's losing it.

"Never mind, Peter. Your mother-in-law's right." Laura pushes him toward our car. She's probably wondering how she ended up here with all of us. I snicker inside. Mom managed to break them up after all.

Dad sits next to the chauffeur, his neck as straight as if he's swallowed an ice pick. "Well, guys," he says, and nothing else. He does this a lot these days. He'll start a sentence and after the first two words forget what he wanted to say. Grandma sits in the back next to Luuk and me. She's trembling so violently I can feel it through the seat.

"Where's Kim?" she asks Dad.

"In the other car."

"Is it really necessary for that poor girl to ride with those people?" All her anger is compressed into those last two words.

"Listen, Tineke," Dad says without looking back. "It's about Jet today. Not about you and your annoyances. Let's try to keep things civil."

"Don't you start on about civility now."

Mom would be in stitches.

We drive slowly through the bleak, silent streets of South Amsterdam. Cyclists stop for us; some pedestrians take off their hats. Other cars join the procession. I feel like I'm watching a film of my life. None of it is real. I can't even feel sad, though this is the moment for me to do so. Luuk cries the entire drive. He looks ill.

"Are you feeling alright?" I ask.

He shakes his head. Good thing I have another one of Chonk's baggies in my purse. I hand it to him just in time. I rub Luuk's back as he quietly throws up in the bag.

A lot of people with serious faces are waiting for us at the cemetery. We get out without speaking. The men dressed in black take Mom's coffin out of the car and place it on some kind of bed on wheels. The family is then handed a wreath, and we follow the coffin into the auditorium. I didn't know Mom knew so many people. I don't think she knew either.

I look for a familiar face in the crowd. Grandma holds my hand and Luuk's. We're in the front row. There's a life-size photo of Mom on the stage that was taken during that disastrous family vacation, when Mom and Dad thought they'd be fine traveling together despite the divorce. It was taken before Dad decided to admit he had a new girlfriend. Mom's shoulders are bare and brown, she's smiling, and her cheery eyes are looking at us. That's the Mom she used to be, when she still had hope. I see it now, as I did then: How she was convinced she could win Dad over again. How she did her best to be the prettiest, sweetest, and nicest. There's both hope and despair in this image. I think Dad chose this photo because he sees the same thing in it. He's forgotten, but somewhere deep inside, he still loves her.

It's dead quiet. Occasionally, someone whispers or sniffles. Luuk sits by me with his eyes on his shoes. Grandma gets a packet of tissues from her purse. She gives me one as a precaution, but I don't feel like I'm going to cry.

Dad gets behind the lectern and takes out a piece of paper from his inside pocket. His hands tremble. When he begins to speak, a high,

The Grown-Up

shrill squeal fills the room. A man in black runs onto the stage and hastily fumbles with the wiring.

"Dear, dear friends and family of Jet's. Dear, dear Jet. I know you're not waiting for a speech from me. We fought like cats and dogs these last years. Since your passing, I've been blaming myself, every single day."

"Oh God, he's not going to talk about himself, is he?" Grandma whispers.

"You were a beautiful woman. A wonderful mother. An excellent therapist to many. You helped others even when you needed help yourself. But you preferred not to talk about that. You refused to call on anyone, to lean on anybody else. I realized too late your criticisms of me were actually a cry for help. I let you down, and I'll need to learn to live with that. Our dear children . . ." His voice breaks. He rubs his eyes.

"This man," Grandma sighs.

"Stop it," I whisper.

"Our dear children are going to miss you so much, dear Jet. And so am I. But I promise I'll take good care of them. Like you did. Unconditionally, patiently, lovingly. I'll always put them first." He takes a breath. "Now I'd like to hand the microphone to our daughter, Lies."

Behind the lectern, I nearly black out for a moment. My heart is racing, and my jaw trembles so badly I'm afraid I won't be able to get a word out of my mouth. But then all of a sudden I become calm.

"Mom," I say.

Everyone sniffles.

"Luuk and I can't do this without you. If anyone knew that, it was you. You made mistakes, but that was because you were sad when Dad left us. You needed to reinvent yourself. Start a new life on your own. And just when it seemed you were succeeding, it ended. Everyone here thinks you took your own life. Just like Grandpa. I don't believe that."

Whispers, coughing, people shuffling back and forth in their seats.

"Above all else, you were our mother, and you'd never leave us by choice. I believe someone's responsible for your death. Some may take comfort in thinking you went the same way as your father, but I don't. And I promise I'll find the truth. Dear Mom, I love you. I miss you. I need you. And so does Luuk. I hope you've found peace now. You don't need to worry. Luuk and I will be alright.

"Now we're going to play a song you used to sing every day in the kitchen. I thought it was cheesy, but it always made you cry. We're crying with you now. Love you, Mom."

I find it odd that I'm still not crying, even with everyone around me in tears. Grandma rocks back and forth, holding Luuk against her chest. Dad looks almost gray, and Laura's shivering. I see how Dad's hand seeks hers and how she avoids it. The whole room feels like it's trembling, like a mirage. I push my fists against my bladder. It's burning again.

Everyone falls silent when we walk in. The space is called the coffee room, but it's actually a soulless space with hideous paintings of clouds. The people stare at us with stern, fearful, sympathetic eyes as we're shown to some kind of platform where there's a row of chairs waiting alongside a table with a cake and sandwiches next to it.

"How wonderful of Kim to arrange all this," Grandma whispers. Who the fuck cares?

We line up next to each other. This is my first funeral, so I have no idea how to go about anything. "Now all these people will come shake our hands," Laura tells Luuk, who's seized on the sandwiches. "It's called offering your condolences."

A man asks if we want coffee. Luuk wants a Coke, and I ask for tea, hoping I can drink away my rising bladder infection. I feel a pain in my side, and my feet hurt because my dress shoes are too tight. I'm hungry too, though surely you're not supposed to be when burying your mother. Before the drinks are served, Mom's neighbor comes up to us. She's one of those types who ignores queues and boldly does whatever she likes.

The Grown-Up

"Oh, sweetie, my condolences!" she says, sniffling. She just keeps shaking my hand with that clammy hand of hers, until she pulls me toward her and presses a stale armpit in my face by way of a hug. She starts telling Grandma how terrible it all is and how awful she feels for the children especially. Her timid husband follows suit, shaking our hands with his own frail one. He offers his condolences with downcast eyes, as if sadness were contagious. Behind him, an endless chain of people forms. There are teachers from my school, classmates with their mothers and fathers. But some are complete strangers: former friends of Mom's, colleagues of Dad's, Grandma's bridge partners, great-aunts and -uncles I've only heard of before this, people Mom knew from walking the dog in the park or working out at the gym, her clients and former clients. I take in all their faces. Could her Tinder matches be among them? Jochem's here too. He compliments me on my speech.

"Let's meet up again this week," he says. "Because it's clear you're not satisfied with the outcome of our investigation. We'll go through everything step by step once more."

I say I think that's a good idea. He's still really handsome. I might give him Mom's document. Once I feel ready to let go of it.

Next in line is Jan, the colleague Mom had sex with, here with his wife. I can't look her in the eye.

I watch us pass people on to one other like we're on an assembly line, though Luuk's pulled out already and is now playing on his phone. We take people's hands, we smile, we nod, we avoid meeting eyes looking to see our pain. We allow strangers to touch us, comfort us. We pretend to be comforted.

And then there it is: a large, strikingly soft hand with a gold signet ring. A hand that has never worked a single day of hard labor. I look up. A man with a trimmed beard and a black cap stands before me.

"Could you take that off?" I hear Grandma say. "It's not respectful!" She points to the cap.

The man chuckles. His teeth gleam. He takes off his cap. Dark blond, medium-length hair. We look at each other.

"My condolences. You're very well-spoken." He smells of expensive eau de toilette.

"Who are you?" I ask, but I already know.

"Fred," he answers.

"How do you know my daughter?" Grandma sounds like a distressed bird, as if subconsciously she feels something too.

"I'm a former client."

"Ah."

I have to say something too, but I don't know what. "Did you think my mother was a good therapist?" I finally ask. He's started to move on already but turns around.

"Your mother was excellent. Champions League. You can all be really proud of her."

New people move up as he steps away. People with new names and new words of comfort. Grandma looks at me.

"Why are you shaking, Lies? Are you alright?" she whispers.

"I have to go really bad," I say. My bladder feels like it's filled with fire.

"Well, go then, sweetie. Are you having trouble again?"

I nod.

"Oh dear. Should I come with you?"

"Please, Grandma, are you kidding? I'll be fine."

I search through the crowd of people wearing funeral black, but I can't find him. He probably left right away. Why the fuck did he come in the first place? To gloat over what he did? I squeeze through the crowd, avoiding people's pats of encouragement. Who was it who decided it's okay to go around touching people's next of kin?

I run outside, where the smokers are. I feel I've wet my pants a bit. Mees is standing by a planter with some of our classmates. He raises his hand, but I can't stop. Another funeral procession approaches on the other side of the building. This place is a funeral factory, apparently. I hear people say, "That's her daughter," but I continue on past the bicycles in the rack, across the white gravel to who knows where. The

The Grown-Up

parking lot. My lungs are burning in my chest, and my crotch pulses and feels like it's on fire. When I finally reach the large gate in front of the cemetery, I see lots of people get in and out of cars, but none of them are wearing a cap. I pause to catch my breath.

I missed him.

I take a painful pee in a dry ditch behind the poplars that separate the parking lot from the road. I then pull my panties back up, then my stockings, and I straighten my dress. I walk back through the parking lot, shivering a bit from the cold. My bladder hurts really bad, and I'm afraid I'll get a fever. In my head, I talk to myself in the way Mom would. *Look after yourself first. Have a few glasses of water. Grandma surely has some acetaminophen. And go by the medical center this evening. It's going to be alright. It probably wasn't even him. And even if it was, what would you say to him? What would you do? You're no match for him. He's dangerous. Just take that document to the police already. You've put it off long enough. Take care of your brother. He can't afford to lose you too.*

A black Audi slowly drives past and stops a little farther down. The door swings open. For a second, I think it's the police since they always drive black Audis, at least on TV.

I walk over to the car and lean forward to see who's behind the wheel, hoping it's Jochem.

"Get in," God says.

30.

He drives fast past the tall trees lining the road, a row of houses, until our surroundings turn green with only a farm here and there.

"So you're the daughter," he says.

"So you're the murderer," I say.

"Don't you get smart with me."

He's smaller than I'd imagined. His beard is starting to go gray.

"Why are you kidnapping me?" I ask.

He chuckles. It feels like I already know him because of Mom's story. His laugh, his fake toughness.

"You got in," he points out.

"Where are we going?"

"For a drive. For a little chat."

"Are you going to kill me too?"

He bursts out laughing and then throws me a quick glance. I see what Mom meant by "eyes like glowing coals."

"The minute I saw you up there giving your speech, I thought to myself: *This girl has a wild imagination. Just like her mother.*"

"Mom told me everything about you," I lie.

"I seriously doubt that. She was doing her damnedest to keep you and your brother away from me."

"She told me the night before she went missing."

The car's a mess. There are McDonald's bags, empty plastic cups, and half-empty water bottles everywhere. God's face twitches restlessly.

The Grown-Up

"You know what I think would be a good idea?" he says. "If we could just be honest with each other."

"Fine, let's do that. Why are you taking me, and what happened to my mom?"

His hands grip the wheel tightly as he accelerates even more. Is this how things went down with Mom? I should be afraid. But in this moment, all I feel is relieved to be closing in on the truth.

God keeps silent. I can see him thinking. He'd almost gotten away with it, but now he's saddled with me. Did he order me into the car on a whim? He doesn't seem to have any idea what to do with me.

He takes a right and drives up a bumpy dirt road. He doesn't slow down at all.

"It kind of stands out, how fast you drive," I say.

"We're almost there," he says. His phone rings. He puts it on speaker. It's a woman speaking a language I don't understand. God answers in the same language. I could scream for help right now, but I'm afraid of what would happen to me if I did.

"That was Beijing," he says after ending the call. He seems proud that he got to show me he speaks Chinese. "I'm heading there next week."

"Are you going to kill me too?" I ask again.

He gives me a distressed look.

"I didn't kill your mother," he says.

We stop at a vacant lot next to a canal surrounded by tall trees and dense shrubs. It's started to softly rain again. God gets a bottle of water from behind his seat and asks me if I want some. I nod. I need water. I also have to pee again. But I can't let him out of my sight. He puts his seat back and rests his feet on the dashboard. He then stares out in front of him as he takes a pack of cigarettes out from the inside pocket of his leather jacket. "Don't worry," he says. "I'm a dry smoker."

We're silent a long time, as if we're each considering what to do next. There's no turning back now. He's more or less kidnapped me, even though I chose to come along. How do I get out of this? How can we both get out with what we need?

I tell myself he's looking for some kind of forgiveness. But I know better. He has no choice but to get rid of me. And me? I'm looking for the final piece of Mom's story. I don't want her to be remembered as some unstable madwoman who abandoned her kids.

"Listen," he says all of a sudden. "I was seriously crazy about your mother. And that doesn't happen to me very often. I always say: I have a lot of women, but who has me? Well, believe me, your mother had me."

I drink some water, trying to relax the muscles in my abdomen. The pain is getting worse. My head is warm, my body cold.

"Why my mother? Out of what must have been hundreds of women? Why Mom, who has kids, and who already suffered so much?"

"You shouldn't underestimate your mother." He puts his hand against his forehead. "I thought, *What if I started dating smart women?* Psychologists, psychiatrists, lawyers. To learn from them, and to test out my theories."

"Why do all that?"

"I had a plan. I want to know how this thing works." He taps his finger against his skull. "I love it," he says. "The brain, how it works, how it can be influenced. I'm studying psychology because I'm fascinated by the question of whether people have free will or not. What makes us do what we do? How can we control our constantly swirling thoughts? Is behavior learned or genetically predetermined? Those sorts of things. That's how I met your mother on a dating site. She looked smart. And sweet. And she was a psychologist. Our first date, wow. It was almost like . . . an explosion. Like we were able to read each other. I knew right away: This is my woman. We're soulmates. But was I ready for this? Could I handle it? Because she was something else. Pretty. Independent. Far more intelligent than me. What was I supposed to do?"

"A fascinating story," I say. "But I really need to pee. Do you think that's possible?"

"Do whatever you have to, missy. You're free to go anytime."

The Grown-Up

I get out and look for a place where I can pull my tights down privately. There's some kind of corrugated metal shed to the left between the trees. I walk around it. The rain has stopped. Everything is completely silent. It strikes me that no one will ever find us here. I roll up my dress and squat. The pain is intense, but familiar too. I look in front of me, past the canal. In the distance, on the other side of an expansive pasture, are some houses. If I dive into the canal, I can get to the other side and run to them.

Do it, Mom says in my head. I roll up my panties and stockings and see I've peed blood. Why am I cursed with an ailment that messes up everything? As I straighten my dress, I hear someone take in a breath. Loudly, like he's just been working out.

"There, on the opposite side where those houses are. That's where it happened."

"Are you spying on me?"

"Were you planning to make a run for it?"

I'm breathing hard now too, from fear and from pain. "Is that where you killed her?"

"I didn't kill her. She was alive when I left." He looks at me, horrified. His expression pleases me.

"Right. That's why you bothered to erase your tracks, wipe her computer, her phone."

"Fine, smarty-pants, don't believe me. Run along home, then. I didn't wipe anything, didn't kill anyone, none of that. Go on! I'm done with this." God turns and walks back to the car. He gets in and starts the engine. I give him the finger.

He drives off, slowly at first, hoping I'll run after him, which of course I don't. Only once he's fully out of sight does it hit me. Is he really leaving me out here? Did I let him get away—and get myself abandoned in the middle of nowhere, all because I had to be an idiot and act tough? I didn't even take note of his license plate. I don't know where I am or how to get out of here. By the time I'm able to report him to the police, he'll have gotten away, probably to China. I reject the idea that he might have told me the truth. I blow on my cold hands to warm them. Just as I start to walk in a random direction, I hear a car.

I was right. The loser's coming right back. With screeching tires. He drives so fast the car looks like it's levitating. Even though he's getting closer, he keeps accelerating. It takes a few seconds for me to realize he's headed straight at me. I jump out of the way and step back until I begin to sink in the mud around the canal. I try to pull my feet out, but I only sink down deeper. The car skids to a halt right in front of me. I hear the door open and shut. I'm completely stuck.

He bursts out laughing, the sadist. "You should've seen yourself!" He roars with laughter, his voice high and shrill. "You really thought . . ." He walks toward me. I'm crying now. He reaches down and holds out a hand. "Come on, little one, just take it."

I don't have much of a choice.

He pulls my arm until I hear a plopping sound and feel my feet come loose, and he then reels me in like a giant fish.

"You'll get sick like this," he mumbles.

I sit in the grass, shaking. My shoes are still in the mud. He walks to his car, opens the trunk, and comes back with a gray towel that smells of men's sweat, and a black jogging suit.

"Put this on."

I change behind the shed. The thought of having to wear his filthy exercise clothes makes me sick. Then I hear him tug at the shed's door.

"Look what we have here," he cries.

Inside are two stools and a small woodstove. An assortment of fishing rods and a large net hang from the walls. God throws two pieces of wood in the stove, then some crumpled-up newspapers and kindling, and lights a fire.

"I want to go home," I say.

"You need to warm up first," he says.

"My father's probably out looking for me."

"Sure he is."

The Grown-Up

I hold my hands and feet to the fire. There's a hammer hanging to the right of me, and an axe next to it. I visualize the move in my head: jump up, take two steps, grab the hammer, strike. I don't drink any more of the water God gave me. He's trying to unsettle me by acting really kind.

"Alright. Can we talk now without you getting all dramatic?"

I nod.

"I'm not going to kill you."

"You tried to kill me already."

"I was just goofing around. If I'd wanted to get rid of you, I could've easily drowned you. Do you think I'm crazy or something?"

"Yes. That's exactly what I think."

"Would you shut up and listen for a minute?" He presses his hands against his temples. "Do you know I can't stop thinking about that night? Do you have any idea how shitty I feel?"

"You feel shitty? You? You really are a narcissist."

"That's enough. I'm going to tell you something, and I want you to listen. You can decide what you think about it afterward." He closes his eyes.

Jump up, take two steps, grab the hammer, strike. Don't miss. There's a fire raging in my crotch.

"That dress you're wearing, your mother bought it in London. She showed it to me, and she looked so happy . . . She loved you very much. I could see it in her eyes. I'll admit I felt a bit jealous. I realized that no matter how wild we were about each other, she'd never look as happy telling someone about *me*. She'd never be so unconditionally crazy about me as she was about you. And your brother, of course."

I want to tell him it's crazy to be jealous of a mother's love for her children.

"No, don't say anything." He puts his hand over my mouth before I can speak. "We had something in common, your mother and I. We're both wounded. Her father killed himself, my mother was severely depressed. We recognized that wound in each other instantly. It's said everyone you meet can teach you something if you let them. I knew right away: She and I could learn a lot from each other. We could help each other."

"You wanted her to save you."

He puts his fingers in his ears. "When we made love, it was almost like fighting. We went straight for each other's wounds. It frightened me. Your mother too. I wanted her all to myself. But she had you, your brother, your father, Jan. There was always someone else coming between us, and she didn't want to tell anyone about us. I didn't know it was possible to become that obsessed with a woman. I had to have her. I thought: How do I get inside that head of hers? How do I make her wholly mine?"

I get the feeling he's talking to himself.

"And then she broke up with you," I say, trying to get him back on track.

"She kept breaking up with me. I did the same with her. It became a way of manipulating each other. I didn't take any of it seriously. The only thing I took seriously was the fling she had with that colleague of hers, Jan. That didn't make any sense. She'd lied about it, so I started following her."

"You do know what you're saying is sick?"

God shakes his head, closes his eyes again. "It's sick that acting this way became necessary. That's what lies do."

It scares me just how convinced he is that this is true.

"The last time we met, she broke up with me yet again, but this time it was different. The way she said it. The way she wouldn't look directly at me. When she finally did, I saw it in her eyes. Just like that, she was a stranger again. You don't yet understand how brutal and strange that is. Feeling, one moment, that you've fully merged with another, and the next moment, finding yourself discarded. I lost my mind a bit as a result."

Despite the heat coming from the fire, I'm ice cold.

"If only she'd let me in, if she'd accepted me as I am, if she'd opened herself up to me a little more . . ."

"So it was all her fault."

"She seemed quite laid-back, but she wasn't at all."

"Hey, asshole, you're talking about my mom here. Who you murdered. She's the most beautiful person I've ever known. She had more love and decency in her little finger than you have in your entire body."

"You don't know me at all, and you didn't know her as well as you thought."

"I don't see why you're trying to convince me my mom was no good. She's dead, you're alive. Just tell me what happened without blaming her and acting like we should feel sorry for you."

He turns toward me. His eyes are bloodshot. His lips form a straight line. "Shut up! I'm serious. I only wanted what's best for her, dammit! What didn't I do for her? London! The Ritz! The most expensive hotels, the best champagne, tables in the fanciest restaurants. That cottage over there, so we could be together more often. I could have gone to China instead. Plenty of women there would love those kinds of things."

"You registered the house in her name."

"I had to. I'm not a resident of the Netherlands, so renting a house here in my name would be asking for trouble, in terms of taxes."

"You were stalking her online the whole time, not just toward the end."

"Well, 'stalking.' Who doesn't these days, with all this social media? It was more a kind of game. I was in love, and people in love do such things. You want to possess the other person, know everything about her, watch her every step. But how do you know all of this?"

"Mom wrote everything down from the beginning. I know everything. I even saw your dirty movies."

God gets up and opens the door of the shed further.

"So did my best friend, by the way," I go on. "So whatever you're planning to do with me, he knows you exist. He can prove you were with Mom that last night," I bluff. "If anything happens to me, he'll take it to the police."

He kicks at the ground. "If you had it, you'd have turned it over long ago."

"I *should* have turned it over long ago."

"That video doesn't prove a thing. Except that your mother was into it."

I jump up, take two steps, pull the hammer from the holder, and lunge. He catches my arm with one of his hands. His other has me by the throat. He knocks my leg out from under me, but the woodstove breaks my fall. I feel the heat of the fire against my side, and my dress starts to smoke as the hammer slips from my fingers. He grips me by the arms while I thrash around, trying to kick his legs.

"Will you stop? I'll let go but only if you calm down, understand?"

I nod, eyeing the hammer, which is now on the ground between the two stools. God kicks it away, toward a pile of old clothes next to the door.

"Get a grip, for God's sake. You really are like your mother."

"Take me home," I gasp. I feel his grip loosen.

"Can I really let go of you? You'll stay calm now?"

"Yes, please. Come on."

"Alright. Sit down and shut up."

He puts me on the stool. It's wet between my legs. I've peed my pants.

"Before I take you home, you have to promise me one thing."

"Whatever you say."

He stays silent a long time. God can claim I'm free to go whenever I want, but that's not how it feels. He's unpredictable and acts like someone who could explode at any time. Back in the car, I felt relieved I'd found him, knowing I'd finally get the truth. Only, that relief's now

The Grown-Up

given way to regret and fear for my life. This isn't what Mom wanted. I need to stay with Luuk. I need to finish my life.

"No, not *Whatever you say*. I want you to actually believe me. I really didn't kill your mother. I know I was seemingly the last person with her, but when I left her she was alive. And she had my phone. She could have called a taxi, or someone else, like you. Did anyone find a phone?"

"No."

"See? The phone is gone, that proves it."

"If your phone had been found, that hardly would have been to your advantage. She did leave a note, though. The police see it as a goodbye letter, but I think . . ."

"She'd left the note on her pillow. When I woke up, she wasn't in bed beside me. That's when I found it. I couldn't handle it."

"What did you do?" I ask.

"Nothing," he says.

"We said we wouldn't lie. Tell me what really happened."

"She slipped in the bathroom."

"After you pushed her."

"Yes." He stares at his fingernails. "I didn't really push her, not hard. I just didn't want her to leave. Not that way, like a thief in the night. I tried to grab her and she slipped. Bam. Her head against the sink. It scared the hell out of me. I wanted to help her, but she wouldn't let me touch her even though she was all banged up."

"So then you put her in the tub."

"I went to bed first. *Screw this*, I thought. *If you're done with me, then just go.* But a few hours later, she was still lying there, and by then I wasn't angry anymore. I then put her in the bath. I know it's hard to understand this dynamic between us. In that moment, I understood too that it would be better if we went our separate ways. But that's how it always went: as soon as one of us wanted to leave, the other would give chase like crazy."

"I need to see a doctor," I say. "I'm getting a fever."

He puts his hand against my forehead. "You're ice cold."

"Will you please take me to a doctor?" My lower back is aching.

"Do you believe me now?" he asks.

"Yes," I say, to be done with it. But he's not done.

"Okay, listen," he says. "I did give her two oxycodone pills."

"Why?"

"Do you have any idea how often I ask myself that? If that might have had anything to do with her dying? What was I thinking?"

I can't stand how sincere he sounds.

"I think I didn't want her to leave, for it to end. I thought: *I just need to get her to calm down.* You know, we really loved each other, but it was like we were out of sync. We needed to start over. At least, that's how I felt at the time. We needed to shed our old habits, free ourselves from our demons. I wanted to leave, I wanted to stay. I wanted to hold her, and I wanted to fight with her. I wanted to protect and possess her, and she wanted . . . I don't know what. Her ex, I think. Your father. She felt about him the way I felt about her."

God's insinuating himself into my mind and planting his toxic seeds.

"Then suddenly your mother completely lost it, just when I'd gotten her to settle down. She smashed a chair through the window, ran outside naked. That's when I finally thought, *Screw this, I'm out of here.* I took off but left a phone behind for her to use. That was all. She was totally unhinged."

I get up and lean against the corrugated wall.

He stands up right behind me. "Are you alright?"

I squat, grab the hammer, turn around, and swing. I hit him too low. He jumps on me and drags me outside, where it's now pouring down rain.

"Get ahold of yourself, kid!" he cries, panting.

The Grown-Up

He pushes me to the ground, and I roll out from underneath him. Once more, I lunge with the hammer. He dodges it and grabs my arm. The hammer falls from my hands.

He sits on top of me with his knees on my arms. "The apple doesn't fall far from the tree," he says. "You've got the same fighting spirit."

His weight presses down on my ribs. I see dark gray skies, grass, his furious expression. From below, his face looks flabby. I try to push him off me, to hit his back with my knees, but it's no use. When I try to scream, he covers my mouth.

"I messed up with your mother that night. I gave her those pills because she was acting hysterical. Like you are now."

I try to bite his fingers.

"It's the truth. I panicked. Now will you stop?"

I turn my head. His hand is against my nose. I can hardly breathe.

"You don't understand, little girl, because you haven't known great love yet. Calm down!"

I manage to wriggle my left arm free from under his knee. I think of Luuk, Dad, Grandma. I can't die here. They'll never get over it.

"Listen! I'm sorry about all of it. It keeps me up every night! I did everything wrong, but I didn't murder her!"

I feel around in the damp soil, the grass, until I feel something smooth.

"Then who did?" I scream.

His grip loosens.

"Someone else. All my things were still there. My phone too. I was afraid to go back. Look at me!"

I look him in the eye. He wants me to forgive him.

"When I heard her body was found, I thought: *This is it. They'll find my things, my phone, our photos, everything. I'm fucked.* But then nothing happened. That's why I'm sure someone was there. I don't believe she killed herself either. That's what I wanted to tell you. But I didn't do it. Are you listening?"

"Don't lie," I say. I raise my arm. I watch the hammer. How it flies through the air. How it connects with his temple. How blood gushes out. How his eyes pinch closed. How his mouth opens and then closes. How his cheeks move. How I hit him again, and again. I keep striking at him until his body falls like a weight on me and stops moving.

I walk. It takes forever, but I'm finally able to stop a car. The driver hands me her phone. I call the only number I know by heart. Dad's so happy to hear my voice he cries.

31.

I stumble, fall, and get back up. I need to keep moving, away from here, away from God. It's only after I've climbed up the bank of the canal and slipped that I notice he hasn't come running after me. I hide behind a tree and wait. No one comes. I feel disappointed for a second. He's let me go. "What the fuck?" I mutter to myself. Now what? Is this another one of his sick pranks? Is he waiting for me back at the cottage, laughing?

You're so confused, Twigs. His voice, everywhere.

I think of my children at home by themselves. How they'll wake up soon and I won't be there.

It's cold and I'm shivering so bad I can hear my own teeth chatter. *Take care of yourself, no one else will. Set clear boundaries; it's the best thing for the other person too. Fear is suppressed anger. You're not afraid of what others might do but of what you're capable of yourself.* All the therapeutic bullshit advice I give every day rushes through my head. *If you don't know what to do anymore, then calmly sit and talk to yourself like you're your own best friend.*

Alright, Jet, tell me: What should I do now?

Go back. Check and see if there's anyone at one of the other houses.

But I'm naked. They'll think I'm crazy.

So what? And let's be honest, you are crazy. You let things go too far, despite everything you know. But you've hit rock bottom. Things can only get better from here.

I'm so scared I can hardly move.

Come on. You need to get up. One step at a time.

I'm standing. One hand covering my breasts, another in front of my privates.

Look, you can walk around the field through the trees.

What if he's out there waiting for me?

Is that what you think? Or what you're hoping for? For him to welcome you with a blanket and say he's so sorry?

I shake my head and walk behind the shrubbery.

You do realize you have to call the police, don't you?

I want it to be over. I'm not calling anyone.

Yes you are. You're reporting him. He hurt you. Drugged you. Raped you.

Isn't that an exaggeration?

He ravaged you.

I ravaged him too.

Just look at yourself.

You don't understand.

Yes I do.

He didn't rape me. I wanted it.

I reach the holiday cottages at last. The first house I see is abandoned. There's a dirty tablecloth on the plastic outdoor table.

Go on, wrap yourself in that.

From behind the conifers, I stare at our house for several minutes. I think he left.

How can you be sure?

It feels deserted.

You hope he's still here, don't you?

No I don't.

Except I do. The unhealthy half of me does.

I creep through the garden, grab a rusty rake I just manage to avoid stepping on, and finally reach the sliding door I smashed to pieces. I step inside armed with the rake. No one's in the living room. His coat, his scarf, and all my clothes are still here. Our half-full glasses of wine are on the table. Barefoot, I proceed with caution, avoiding the shards of glass.

"Hello?"

Don't do this. Be quiet. Listen.

For a moment, I think I hear him breathing.

It's in your head.

I check the bedroom. The bathroom. Everything's just as it was when I left. He was apparently in as much of a hurry to leave as I was.

Either that, or he's coming back.

My clothes are next to the bed.

Don't shower first, just get dressed!

I'm overcome by everything that happened last night. Him washing me in the bath. His body on top of mine. The despair and rage in his eyes.

I lean the rake against the wall and fall onto the bed. I don't think I've ever felt this lonely.

Come on, dummy, stay with me. We have to get the hell out of here.

I see his phone on the nightstand, connected to the charger.

He's coming back.

Get out!

I grab the phone. He's disabled the screen lock, which means I can use it. Is this a trap? Is he watching me? I put the phone back. He's everywhere. I get up and want to run away, but my knees are too weak and I fall.

You're not going to die. Now, come on. Get up. Let's go!

I can't do it. My legs are weak as cooked spaghetti. I pull myself back up on the bed, grab the phone again, and dial the only number I know by heart.

"Help me," I say.

32.

"Goddammit, Jet." He drags me across the room by my arm and flings me onto the bed. "What's going on? Are you on something?"

I shake my head.

He slaps my face. I look into the eyes that are so familiar to me, which used to look at me so differently. Now he despises me.

"Alright. Tell me what happened. Do I need to call an ambulance? Why'd you call me anyway? All you had to do is call emergency services. Is this another one of your cries for attention?"

"Where are the children?"

"They're supposed to be with you!"

"Didn't I ask you to pick them up?"

"You asked no such thing. They're probably still asleep. Or do you have them . . . Jet?" His thumb and index finger squeeze my jaw. "Out with it," he says.

Bitch. I'm not sure if he actually says that part, but he definitely thinks it.

He takes a breath. "Look, Jet, I'm going to make coffee, and you're going to clean yourself up. And then you're going to tell me what happened."

I hate the way he always gives people orders, but I know he's doing what's right now. We have a common interest in the kids, so I do what he says. I shower, brush my teeth. I'm starting to get a grip again.

The Grown-Up

He's the last person you should have involved in this, Jet. How did you think this was going to go? What were you thinking? That you'd have some romantic reconciliation? Why do you always show these men your helpless side? Is it because they enjoy saving you so much?

I dry myself, get dressed, and feel myself calm down. This is a turning point. I'm not going to argue with him.

"Thank you" is the first thing I say.

He hands me a cup of coffee. "I'm going to call Laura and have her pick up the kids."

"No," I say. "Just take me home or let me call them."

The coffee is insanely strong.

"You don't think I'm leaving them with you in this state, do you?" He laughs scornfully. I take another sip.

"Like you never left them alone for a few hours." In fact, he did it every Tuesday evening, while I was doing group therapy at my practice, in order to fuck that whore.

"That was a bit different."

He's right about that. He always left a note. *Dad's at the neighbors' house. Call me if you need me.* Once, Lies had a bladder infection, and she called him. He rewarded her with an iPhone for not saying anything to me about it.

"How did you even end up here? Some man, right? Looks like the two of you had a real time of it."

"Can we get going before he comes back?"

"Are you afraid of him?"

"Yes."

"That's the kind of person you let into your life? As a mother?"

"Please, Peter, this isn't the time."

"There's glass everywhere. What did he do to you? Or maybe you did it to him? Next thing I know there'll be a body around here. I don't want to be an accessory to anything."

I hate him when he acts like this, like he's so outraged. He never changes.

"Are you depressed again?"

"No."

He paces the room, gloating over his position as the upright parent. "I'm going to have to report this."

"Can't we just be sweet to each other for once? It has to still be in there somewhere, our love, or friendship at least. You could just say, *Sweet Jet, how awful for you. Come on, I'll take you home. We'll deal with this together. I'll help you.*"

"Is that what you imagined when you called me?"

"I only know one number by heart. Yours."

"And you don't find that pathetic? That you know my number and not our kids'?"

"I wouldn't have wanted to upset them if I did." I feel dizzy. "Did you put something in the coffee?"

"Of course not!" He screams: "My God! Do you see how paranoid you are?" Suddenly his cup whizzes past my ear. "I've had enough of this!" He starts tapping frantically on his phone.

"Don't!" I cry. I leap at him and try to wrestle the phone from his hands.

"You're crazy . . . bitch!"

We're gripping each other's wrists, circling one other. I slip on the glass.

"Keep the kids out of this!" I yell.

He's behind me now, and he's got me pinned.

"You're worthless," he manages to squeeze out.

I kick my feet in the air, searching for his shins, his knees, his crotch. We've fought before this. In fact, we've always fought. Fight for power: God says that's what I do. *Why don't you try surrendering?*

Peter drags me into the hallway. "Knock it off, goddammit!"

I thrash around, gasping for breath. I kick the bathroom door open. He forces me down on my knees. "Will you stop?"

Surrender.

"No."

The Grown-Up

He grabs me by the hair. I try to bite him, and his sweater tears.

"Jet! Stop!"

"You stop! Let go of me!"

His grip weakens momentarily. I turn and knee him directly in the stomach. Then his hands are on my face. I fall backwards into the bathtub, which is still half-full of water. I feel his fingers on my ears, my jaw, the top of my head. He pushes, keeps pushing, and I think I hear him crying.

Only now am I able to do it.

I let go.

EPILOGUE

"What I dream all the time," I tell Mees as we walk along the beach, "is that I run into my mom on a busy street. We both burst out in tears because it turns out she's still been living in our old house all this time. 'You forgot about me,' she sobs, and I try to convince her it's not true, but I can't make a sound."

Mees puts his skinny arm around me. It's oppressively warm out, even though the sun has nearly set. I already know I don't ever want to be without him. I worry every day that he'll suddenly break up with me. Because I'm not that nice to be with. I talk about my mom way too much, and I still get bladder infections all the time. Mees never knows what to say when I bring her up. He just asks, "Do you talk about it with your therapist too?"

Of course I do. Every other Tuesday, from four until half past five. I've also done EMDR therapy. That helped somewhat, because I'm not quite as anxious now. My dreams about God and the blood gushing from his head are less frequent now. It also helped that, after the police read Mom's story and saw the photos, they identified God as her murderer. Even though they never found his stuff, which he claimed he'd left in the house.

"This man knew exactly what he was doing, because he'd taken extreme care to cover his tracks," they said. "There wasn't a fingerprint, not a single trace in the house. We have no camera images, no data from his phone."

The Grown-Up

People called me a hero. I was in all the newspapers, and all the talk shows wanted to have me on as a guest. Someone even planned to make a documentary about me. I turned it all down, though, because I don't feel like a hero. I did what I had to do to survive. But sometimes I wonder if that's actually true. Would he really have killed me? Did he really kill Mom? He must have done it, even if he claimed he didn't. Or if she did it herself, on purpose or by accident, he drove her to it. He wore her out, pressured her, drove her insane. God had a way of getting inside a person's head and screwing them up, and he loved doing it. He did it to me too in those few hours I was with him. He may be dead, but I still hear his voice in my head.

We sit down in the sand. Mees has stolen a bottle of rosé he swiped from his parents. He gets two glasses from his backpack, carefully wrapped in a dish towel. He's perfect, with his perfect parents and perfect manners. That makes him a little boring too, but what the hell, I can do with a bit of boredom. We started officially dating six months ago today.

"How are things at home?" Mees opens the bottle and fills our glasses. We're not alone. The beach is full of people waiting for the sunset. I get out my phone and take a selfie of us. I'm proud to be in a relationship with him. It makes me feel grown-up and secure. I wear a chain with his name around my neck. It feels wonderful to belong to someone.

"Better," I say. "Now that Laura's gone."

This happened two weeks ago. Dad changed after Mom died, and Laura couldn't deal with it. His going from being a divorced man who enjoyed going to festivals and drinking Aperol Spritz to being a mourning, depressed single father couldn't have been easy for her.

"Did you really think she was that awful?"

"Honestly, I kind of liked her toward the end. That's why it's good they separated. She deserves better. She can have kids of her own with a nice young man."

"It's sad for your father, though."

"Yeah."

Dad's completely fallen apart. He wanders the house at night and walks the dog for hours during the day. He took leave from his office, saying he was overworked. Sometimes he stands by my bed in the middle of the night and stares at me. I pretend I'm sleeping. Luuk told me Dad does the same with him.

"But he's super nice to us. He lets us do practically anything. He cooks whatever we want. Sometimes he hugs us for no reason. He'll watch *The Voice* with us and stock up on candy beforehand. We've even convinced him that we should all move back to Mom's house."

"Awesome! You'll live close by again!"

"He said, *I think that's exactly the punishment I deserve,* which I thought was a bit odd. I think Mom's death made him realize everything he did wrong and that he actually misses her a lot. So now he'll live in her house and be reminded of her every day. But it's what Luuk and I want. Everything we still have of Mom is there."

The rosé is a bit sour, but we keep drinking. I love how numb I feel. We kiss, much more naturally than we did in the beginning. Our bodies know one other quite well by now.

"We'll do everything very differently later in life, won't we?" Mees whispers, his nose in my hair.

"Absolutely," I say. I'm happy he's talking about later on in life. In my head, Mom says, *Enjoy it, my sweet girl, and do your best.* So I do. My very best.

ABOUT THE AUTHOR

© 2023 by Philippe Vogelenzang

Saskia Noort is a Dutch writer and columnist whose books have sold 3.5 million copies worldwide. Her novels have been translated into fifteen languages and have been adapted for television, film, and theater. Saskia's thriller *The Grown-Up*, a bestseller in the Netherlands, sold over two hundred thousand copies.

ABOUT THE TRANSLATOR

Jai van Essen was born and raised in the Netherlands and spent time in the United States during his youth. He studied English literature at the University of Amsterdam and has had a lifelong love of language and fiction. Jai is currently based in Amsterdam, where he works as a freelance translator.